J.T. Fernie is the pen name of Moira Macfarlane, British Consul in Florence for eight years and briefly Acting Director of the British Institute of Florence. Her early love of telling stories led her first into teaching, then as an HMI with the former Scottish Office Education Department. Her love of travel and literature enlivened the stories she told to children and friends, allowing free rein to her imagination—a freedom denied in writing educational reports for publication.

Moira returned to Scotland when she retired and, encouraged by her children and happily distracted by her grandchildren, began writing fiction. *The Istanbul Ring* is her first novel.

This book is dedicated to my brilliant mother, Jenny Tasker Fernie, who died too soon, but not before she had inspired me with her story-telling, and to Mike, Helen, Sarah and Jet, for their encouragement and support.

J.T. Fernie

THE ISTANBUL RING

AUSTIN MACAULEY PUBLISHERS™

LONDON • CAMBRIDGE • NEW YORK • SHARJAH

A CIP catalogue record for this title is available from the British Library.

ISBN 9781035811199 (Paperback)
ISBN 9781035811205 (ePub e-book)

www.austinmacauley.co.uk

First Published 2024
Austin Macauley Publishers Ltd®
1 Canada Square
Canary Wharf
London
E14 5AA

I would like to thank staff at Austin Macauley for their trust and prompt acceptance of my first novel. I am very grateful to the production team for their help and advice, in particular staff in the graphics department and my editor. Inspiration for this book came from many sources—happy years bringing up my family with my husband Doug in the Bellevue area of Edinburgh; working in Italy with my wonderful Foreign and Commonwealth Office colleagues; and time spent exploring the wonders of Istanbul and Berlin. I am indebted to Robert Edsel for his inspiring book, 'The Monuments Men'; and to the many historians who have written so movingly about the fall of Berlin and its grim aftermath.

And last, but not least, to my readers.

Table of Contents

Good seemed the world to me who could not stay
The wind of loss that swept my hopes away...
Light of mine eyes and harvest of my heart,
And mine at least in changeless memory!
Ah! When he found it easy to depart,
He left the harder pilgrimage to me!
Oh, camel driver, though the cordage start,
For God's sake, help me lift my fallen load,
And pity be my comrade of the road.
Hafez: 14th century, Persia
Translation: Gertrude Bell...

Principal Characters

In Rome

Angharad Wilson (Anya): First Secretary, British Embassy
Farah Iravani: Persian emigrée and friend of Angharad
Amir Rashid: Consultant Paediatric Oncologist at Bambino
Gesu Hospital
Everett Sympson: HM Ambassador to Italy
Christopher Nutall: Depute Head of Mission, British Embassy
Andrew Blyth: Head of Security, British Embassy, Rome
Dr Soraya Akhtar: Industrial Chemist and undercover agent
for Iranian Intelligence (VAJA)
Kamran Teherani: VAJA agent
Jed Baker: CIA

In Bavaria

Baron Hans Ludvig von Seidel: Wealthy art collector, friend
of Herman Göring
His heirs:
Hans Peter von Seidel: Waffen-SS officer, declared 'missing
presumed dead' in 1946
Hans Dietrich von Seidel: Wehrmacht officer, died Berlin
1945

Stefania von Seidel

Hans Jurgen von Seidel: died aged 8, 1934

Monsignor Hans Albrecht von Seidel: Priest, Art Historian, and friend of Charles Gibson

In Berlin

Hans Dietrich von Seidel: April-July 1945

Hanna Brandt: Nurse, mother of Hans Dietrich's daughter, Magdalena

In Leigh-on-Sea, Essex

John and Sarah Mitchell: Parents of Agnes and Marianne Mitchell

Catherine Mitchell: Daughter of Marianne, brought up by Agnes

In Edinburgh

Marianne Mitchell: 1950–1958

Catherine Mitchell: 1952–1958; and from 1974 onwards

Charles Gibson: Art Historian and friend of Hans Albrecht von Seidel

Chief Inspector John Arbuthnot: Lothian and Borders Police, Serious Crimes Unit

Niall Chambers: Goldsmith

Rosemary and Peter Bruce: New owners of Charles Gibson's former home

In Pergamino, Argentina

Hans Peter von Seidel (known as Pieter Steen): 1945–1987
Maria Silvia Martinez: Young partner of Pieter Steen
Jan Marten: Student admirer of Maria Silvia

In Istanbul

Chief Inspector Kadir Demercol: Serious Crimes Unit,
Istanbul Police
(Bas Müfettiş Kadir Demercol in Turkish. English 'Chief
Inspector' used for simplicity.)
Ayşe Demercol: Wife of Kadir
Inspector Djavid: Serious Crimes Unit, Istanbul Police
Faisal Arslan: Ottoman Art Expert, friend of Niall Chambers
Alfred Fischer (known as Aydin Fenerbaçe: ex-sergeant
Waffen-SS, and associate of Hans Peter von Seidel)

In Mogadishu

Hans Peter von Seidel (alias Pieter Steen, now Per Svensson):
1987–1995

In Glasgow

Reg Manson: Gangland boss
Ron and Rikki Manson: Reg's sons

Chapter 1
Edinburgh, 1993

Lost in thought, DCI John Arbuthnot stood at the window of a Victorian drawing room in Bellevue Avenue, a quiet cul-de-sac at the east end of Edinburgh's fashionable New Town. Incessant rain hammered against the glass, obscuring the view and intensifying the bleakness of his mood. Thirty-seven years of working with major incident teams had not diminished his anger at the pointless taking of life, and this case affected him more than most.

Twenty-four hours had passed since the police had received an hysterical call from Dr Charles Gibson's housekeeper to say that she had found her employer lying on the floor of his study. He had not died easily.

The house had been left in turmoil, but nothing appeared to be missing. The contents of drawers, cupboards and bookshelves were strewn across floors. Flight tickets for Munich and around £500 in deutschmarks lay on Dr Gibson's desk alongside his passport and a wallet containing cash and credit cards.

The housekeeper and two close friends confirmed that his collection of valuable paintings and artefacts appeared to be intact and, thus far, the painstaking efforts of the forensic team had yielded little evidence to go on. John Arbuthnot had the sinking feeling that this murder was the work of professionals who would prove very difficult to trace.

The tabloid press had been quick to link news of another violent death to a recent string of homophobic murders in Edinburgh, but the police had just as quickly ruled that out. Charles Gibson's murder bore none of the grim hallmarks of a homophobic attack. He was fully dressed and in his study. The empty wine bottles, glasses and traces of drugs which had been a feature of the other murders did not feature in this case.

A solitary coffee mug had been knocked over, spilling its contents across the desk before landing on the floor, indicating that Dr Gibson had been at his desk and alone when his assailant or assailants had struck. He had been badly beaten about the head and upper body, and at some stage in proceedings, a paperweight had been used to crush the fingers of his right hand, but there were none of the distinctive trauma injuries found on the other murder victims.

A fatal cardiac arrest had brought his ruthless interrogation to an abrupt and merciful end.

Friends and academic colleagues described him as a gentle, sociable man who had never been known to have a partner of either sex. He had shared his home with his mother until her death a few years previously.

Dedicated to his work, his erudition had been matched by a disarming humility and a total lack of ambition ensuring that he was not caught up in the intense rivalries for power and status, which so often pitched academics against their fellows.

Thus, within twenty-four hours, theft, homophobia, sex and academic rivalry had been ruled out as motives. One potential thread remained. The Bavarian von Seidel family had been the nearest thing Charles Gibson had to a family of his own, and his close friend, Hans Albrecht von Seidel, had been murdered in a hotel room in Istanbul a year before.

Charles Gibson had also been in Istanbul at that time and two unknown men had come looking for him shortly afterwards. The Turkish police were convinced that only the quick thinking of a hotel receptionist had saved Charles Gibson from a similar fate. Sadly, this respite had proved all too short.

There was no doubt in John Arbuthnot's mind that the two deaths were linked. Twelve months earlier, Chief Inspector Kadir Demercol of the Istanbul Directorate of Police had contacted Lothian and Borders Police HQ to ask for help. He believed that Charles may have withheld vital information relating to the death of Hans Albrecht von Seidel and that his life was in danger as a result.

The Turkish police wanted to know if it would be possible for a Scottish detective to ask Charles a few supplementary questions on their behalf, in the hope that he might open up more readily in familiar surroundings than he had in Istanbul in the immediate aftermath of Hans Albrecht's murder.

John Arbuthnot had been less than pleased to find this task on his desk—as if his team didn't have enough to do without running errands for the Turkish police—but Superintendent Markham had been adamant.

"It's important that we cooperate with our international counterparts, and this shouldn't take much of your time—a few questions and a quick report to Chief Inspector Kadir Demercol is all that is required. You should be aware that Demercol is a member of one of the oldest aristocratic families in Turkey."

Arbuthnot had groaned. Why was it that all it took was a grand title to have his super jumping through hoops? To add insult to injury, Markham had just declined a request for additional resources for Arbuthnot's stalled investigation into homophobic attacks in Edinburgh, yet he was prepared to devote valuable police time to assist a foreign force's investigation into the murder of a German—an aristocratic German, needless to say—in Istanbul.

He had left the office muttering under his breath about his super's priorities and whether more manpower might be available to his own team if a homosexual aristocrat assisted by getting himself murdered in Edinburgh.

Rather than bring Charles Gibson into the police station, he had arranged to meet him in the more relaxed atmosphere of the University Staff Club. To his surprise, he had immediately warmed to the gentle man who was still noticeably shocked to the core by his friend's death. At several points during the interview, Charles' eyes had filled with tears and his voice broke as he recalled the strangeness of his last encounter with Hans Albrecht.

However, when Arbuthnot asked why he thought anyone might want to kill Hans Albrecht, Charles became evasive, his professed mystification at odds with his agitated body language. By the end of the interview, Charles was still resolutely maintaining that he had no idea why Hans Albrecht had been murdered, or why the presumed killers had come looking for him next morning.

Arbuthnot was convinced that Charles knew more than he was telling but sensed that further questioning would only add to his distress without prompting further disclosure. He had drawn the interview to a close by advising Charles to change the times and routes of his journeys to and from work and any other regular activity; and to install secure locks at his home.

He had given Charles his card and told him to get in touch immediately if he became aware of any suspicious activity, or if he remembered something that might help the Turkish police. In spite of everything, Arbuthnot had felt sorry for the kindly man who was clearly in possession of a dangerous secret he was too loyal or too afraid to disclose.

He had been told that a German policeman, brought in at an earlier stage by the Turkish Interior Ministry to help with the investigation, had returned to Munich similarly baffled.

International courtesies observed, Superintendent Markham had turned his attention back to matters closer to home and to the furtherance of his career in the brave new world of targets and tight budgets. He had been adamant that Lothian and Borders Police did not have the resource to provide any sort of protection or surveillance for Charles. It was not their case, after all.

No offence had been committed in Scotland. No overt threat to Charles Gibson's safety had been made in Scotland. Charles Gibson had declined the opportunity to explain why he might be at risk. No further police time could therefore be spent on the matter.

A few weeks later, John Arbuthnot had reluctantly agreed to Commander Demercol's request to interview Charles Gibson again, working on the assumption that the murderers must have been seeking an object or information of great value—so great that Hans Albrecht had died to protect it. He said that Hans Albrecht and Charles had been part of an international team of experts studying an important archaeological find at Trebizond on the Black Sea.

Albrecht was a leading authority on Byzantine religious art and Charles on the art and history of the later Ottoman period. Workmen demolishing a site destined for a new mosque had discovered an ancient tomb chamber with frescoes dating back to the 15th century when Venetian merchants had used the building as a Christian church. They had also found the intriguing remains of two women wearing fine Ottoman jewellery dating from a much later period.

As tactfully as he could, DCI Arbuthnot asked Charles if Albrecht had discovered something at the site—something which might have triggered interest in the murky underworld trade in antiquities. However politely put, the implication was not lost on Charles and Arbuthnot remembered his almost apoplectic reaction, "I know why you are asking this, but the question is way out of order! Hans Albrecht's father and oldest brother were known to have dealt in stolen art, but that was a long time ago. Hans Albrecht was just a child at the time, and he dedicated his entire life to trying to redeem his family's reputation. Albrecht became a Catholic priest instead of pursuing a full-time academic career to distance himself from his father and all he stood for."

"It was his way of placing himself beyond his father's control and reach. I can assure you that if Albrecht had found anything of great interest at the Trebizond site, the team leading the excavation would have been the first to know."

Arbuthnot had been at the game long enough to know the difference between genuine indignation and theatrical blustering. He knew that what he had just heard was the former. It left Chief Inspector Kadir Demercol's investigation back at square one. And square one was exactly where John

Arbuthnot now found his own investigation into the death of Charles Gibson.

Charles Gibson's death touched on a raw nerve, because Arbuthnot could not escape the feeling that he had failed the man—failed to gain his trust; failed to persuade him to divulge the secret that had cost him his life; failed to appreciate that the danger was not confined to Istanbul; failed to convince Markham of the need to provide protection for Charles; and failed to check that his home was properly secured and a burglar alarm fitted.

Charles had taken Arbuthnot's advice and strong locks had been fitted to the front door and windows, but the back door was secured by a simple lock that any apprentice housebreaker could have forced with a credit card. It had presented no obstacle whatsoever to professional killers.

Quite by chance, Arbuthnot had encountered Charles again just weeks before his death. He had left police headquarters early that day, following a heated and demoralising meeting with Superintendent Markham on the subject of rising crime rates and missed targets.

It was unusually hot and the walk through Stockbridge to the city centre did nothing to reduce his stress, his way blocked at every turn by hordes of ambling tourists drawn to the city by its International and Fringe Festivals. Seeking refuge from the crowds, the heat and anything that reminded him of work, he decided to have a quick meal at Montpelier's on the south side of town before going home.

He had just ordered when he became aware of a middle-aged man rising from a table of German tourists and approaching him with a beaming smile.

"What a pleasant surprise, Inspector." It was Charles Gibson. "But are you dining alone? You are? Then you simply must join us for dinner and meet Albrecht's family."

"I would be delighted to meet the von Seidel family, but I really shouldn't intrude. I wouldn't be able to contribute much to the conversation, I'm afraid, as I don't speak German."

"Nonsense, nonsense, you would be most welcome, and they all speak excellent English."

Reluctantly, Arbuthnot realised there was no polite way out.

"This is Hanna Brandt, Albrecht's sister-in-law." A tall, handsome woman in her seventies, leant over the table to shake his hand, her severe, angular features softened by dazzling blue eyes and an engaging smile. "And this is Albrecht's niece, Magdalena von Seidel, her daughter, Elsa, and son, Dietrich."

Arbuthnot could not get over how different Charles was surrounded by his adopted family, seeing for the first time the quietly confident, sociable man others had described. After a final attempt to return to his table, Arbuthnot had given in gracefully and joined the family.

When the waiter eventually arrived with the bill, he was astonished to discover that three hours had passed in conversation dominated by interesting tales of the von Seidel family and of Albrecht in particular. At one point, he had asked Charles how he and Albrecht first met.

"Over an exceedingly embarrassing incident in the refectory at Istanbul University thirty-two years ago when I found myself a lira short of the cost of the felafel I had chosen for lunch."

"Uncle Charles had to live on felafel at university because his mother didn't have much money," Dietrich explained in the solemn way of a ten-year-old who knew that not having much money was a serious matter, however remote from his own experience.

Charles continued, smiling wistfully at the memory, "With a hungry queue behind me growing increasingly mutinous, the cashier threatening to call the manager and a frantic search through my pockets revealing no redemptive lira, a quiet voice behind me said, 'Please just add it to my order, this man is my friend'. And so we became, just as soon as I had recovered sufficiently from the embarrassment to introduce myself and thank my new benefactor."

"Charles will never know just how important his friendship was to Albrecht," Hanna said pointedly, looking directly at a blushing Charles. "Albrecht had a wretched time at school. He was ostracised by the other children because his father and oldest brother had been prominent members of the Nazi party and close allies of Hermann Göring."

"To make matters worse, his brother, Hans Peter, had been denounced for countless war crimes. Albrecht rightly thought that Charles needed to know, needed to be free to disengage from the budding friendship if he wanted to. Albrecht could hardly believe it when all Charles said was, 'But you are not your father or your brother'."

"Don't forget, Uncle Albrecht had a very good brother too," Dietrich said, feeling the conversation was getting out of hand and casting his family in a very bad light. "My grandfather, Hans Dietrich, won the Iron Cross and died fighting the Russians in Berlin."

"You must be very proud of your grandfather, Dietrich," Arbuthnot said. "I imagine you have been named after him and I am sure he would have been very proud of you too." Dietrich beamed with pleasure and Arbuthnot skilfully steered the conversation away from war and onto safer ground. Hanna shot him a look of profound gratitude.

Now, staring out at the windswept street below Charles' study window, Arbuthnot pondered the sharp contrast between the frightened, evasive man he had interviewed at the University Staff Club and the relaxed, happy man hosting his family on that enjoyable evening at Montpelier's. If there was a connection between the two murders, why had it taken the killers a year to come calling on Charles Gibson again?

Of course, if all they had known was his name—John seemed to remember being told that a hotel receptionist in Istanbul had refused to give his contact details—then a man called Charles Gibson could have come from anywhere in the English-speaking world and Scotland might not have been the most obvious place to start looking.

A gap of twelve months finally ruled out a link with the excavations at Trebizond; the nationality and professional details of the international experts called to the site would have been easy to check, and Charles would have been found much sooner. Which left the unanswered question of who was behind these murders and why.

A check on Charles Gibson's phone records indicated that he had been at home all evening on the night of his murder. Apart from two late afternoon calls to colleagues and one cancelling a dental appointment, he had made two lengthy telephone calls to Germany during the evening.

Mustering the remnants of his schoolboy German, John called the first number, and the phone was answered by Magdalena von Seidel, Hans Albrecht's much-loved niece, who helpfully switched to English as soon as she heard John's voice and John had the unenviable task of telling her what had happened to Charles.

He heard the horrified, tearful gasp at the other end of the line and asked if she would prefer that he call back later in the day. After a moment or two to collect her thoughts, she reassumed her professional lawyer persona and insisted that they continue.

"Charles and I were discussing arrangements for Stefania's funeral; you remember us talking about Stefania, Albrecht's older sister? She suffered a massive stroke days after news reached us of Albrecht's death and never regained the capacity to speak properly, write or walk again. It was a living nightmare for her and, mercifully, she died two days ago."

"You know we all laughed at her insistence that their oldest brother, Hans Peter, was still alive despite Nazi hunters searching the universe for him after the war. Well, almost the only words she spoke after her stroke were, 'Hans Peter; evil ring—destroy'. She became very agitated when we didn't seem to understand what she was trying to say."

"You know—and don't laugh at this—but I am beginning to wonder if Hans Peter is still alive and somehow behind all this. My mother always half believed that it might be the case. She told me that Hans Peter arrived unannounced as the Russians reached the outskirts of Berlin in 1945 and tried to persuade my father to leave for Portugal with him."

"It was the last anyone in the family saw or heard of Hans Peter, but many Nazis escaped by boat from Portugal to South America. I am glad to say, my father had no need to escape from war tribunals. Sadly though, he did not escape from the Russians."

Similar questions about Hans Peter's possible survival had crossed John's mind, or was he simply clutching at straws? But an 'evil' ring? What ring could be worth killing two men for, assuming it did not hold a diamond the size of the Kohinoor!

Chapter 2
Southend-on-Sea,
October 1995

A biting estuary wind whipped along Southend High Street, sending flurries of late autumn leaves into the air for one last dance before winter's grip froze them to the earth. Overhead vast pyramids of black cloud released cold droplets of rain anticipating the downpour to follow.

A slim figure, huddled into a thin summer coat, hurried along the street towards the warmth of a coffee shop and her weekly indulgence. Here she would linger over a large cappuccino and read one of the newspapers provided free for customers. It had been a frustrating morning, with nothing on offer at the Job Centre and a fruitless search in charity shops for a winter coat.

Fruitless, unless the necessity of keeping warm forced her into reconsidering the purchase of a tweed coat that still bore vestiges of the form and scent of its previous owner. Her last hope was the Oxfam Shop in Southchurch Street which she would check out on her way home.

The frustrations of the day continued. In the café, all that remained of *The Times* was the Sports section and an elderly gentleman at a table in the corner showed no signs of relinquishing *The Independent* any time soon. Forced to consider an alternative, her attention was caught by a headline in *The Sun: 'Murdered Prof—Suspect Released.'*

More than a year had passed since the day when all normality in Angharad Wilson's life had ended; and more than a year since news of the brutal murder of a highly respected Edinburgh academic had reminded her that at least she still had a life. According to the report, a suspect arrested following a televised reconstruction on *Crimewatch* had turned out to be a fantasist.

Police had repeated their appeal to the public for information which might lead them to whoever was responsible for this seemingly motiveless murder.

Bereft of something to read, she stared listlessly at her cappuccino as if somewhere in its depths lay the answer to the devastation of her life. Two years previously, she had been a successful First Secretary at the British Embassy in Rome, living in a large, roof-top flat in Trastevere with breath-taking views across the Tiber to the island on which the Church of San Bartolomeo and its historic hospital dominated the skyline.

Embassy colleagues had wondered at her choice of Trastevere, inconveniently located at some distance from the embassy at Porta Pia, but she loved the area with its quaint cobbled streets and human-sized piazzas. It was the artistic quarter and during the dark years of the fascist regime, had offered a fragile haven for left-wing writers and activists. In many ways, it felt like the authentic heart of Rome, inhabited by real Romans.

The large church in the main piazza, Santa Maria in Trastevere, retained a strong sense of its long history as a place of sanctuary for the community; a sense all but lost in Rome's four more famous basilicas currently over-run by relentless hordes of tourists, the last vestiges of spiritual atmosphere succumbing to mindless chatter, restless, bored children, flashing cameras and the exasperated calls for *SILENZIO* and *NO FLASH* from harassed custodians.

She enjoyed the feeling of being immersed in the local community and her little Vespa had navigated the seven and a half kilometres between home and work with ease.

She thought wistfully of evenings spent watching as the sun sank gently over the Sabine hill spreading a final, kaleidoscopic blaze of colour across the sky before ceding to the velvet dark of a Roman night. She had enjoyed watching as the seasons turned the leaves of the plane trees along the Tiber from the bright green of springtime to the glorious russets of autumn.

She had often thought of the poor and the sick who, in centuries past, had trudged across to Tiberina Island seeking solace and healing from the Fatebenefratelli monks. It had never occurred to her then that one day she, too, would be poor and in need of solace.

Just before her posting to Rome, she had taken out a mortgage on a little Edwardian flat in Golder's Green which would have been waiting for her, mortgage-free, by the time she retired had everything gone to plan. However, even the best of plans can be derailed, and at the age of fifty-two, the derailment of her plans had been as abrupt as it was complete.

She had fallen head-over-heels in love for the first time in her life. There had been other loves of course—a prolonged engagement in her twenties which had not survived her posting to Madrid and his to Islamabad, and several brief affairs, but nothing which had approached the all-consuming intensity of her love for Amir Rashid. A love she had been sure was reciprocated.

Now, two years later, she had no career, no prospect of a new career, no roof-top terrace in Rome, no flat in Golder's Green, no lover and, worst of all, no belief in herself. Home was a small, rented flat in a 60s block behind Victoria Station in Southend-on-Sea. She was unemployed and, apparently, unemployable unless you counted occasional seasonal work in supermarkets.

Making ends meet on benefits was proving to be a challenge and the small amount of money she had received from the sale of her flat was dwindling at an alarming rate. She couldn't help but reflect on the irony of it all—the last coat she had bought had been from the prestigious Italian fashion house, Luisa Spagnoli. Her next coat would be bought from a charity shop in Southend.

Sighing softly, she remembered her grandmother cautioning her that if something seemed too good to be true, it probably was. That pretty well summed up the brief, intense love affair which had ultimately led to her downfall.

The Coat

She saw it at once, prominently displayed in the Oxfam shop window. An elegant, timeless, dark green Loden coat in a size 12; a little too large for her but otherwise perfect. Perfect that was, apart from a price tag of £50. As soon as she entered the shop, a statuesque and rather intimidating volunteer bore down on her; the name badge on her imposing bosom identifying her as Hyacinth.

In response to Angharad's tentative query, she took the coat from the window display extolling its many virtues while steering Angharad towards a mirror where she could see for herself how well it suited her, which it did in every respect apart from costing almost twice the budget she had in mind.

Reluctantly, she slipped the coat off, handing it back to Hyacinth who did little to conceal her exasperation at a customer who had put her to the trouble of dismantling the window display simply to try on a coat she must have known she couldn't afford.

Was it Hyacinth's attitude, or fate, or simply her need of a warm coat that suddenly prompted Angharad to say, "I'll take it!" just as Hyacinth—who bore an uncanny resemblance to her namesake, a television character with grandiose pretensions—was rearming herself for the apparently herculean task of replacing the coat in the window.

"You know this coat is virtually brand new and would have cost at least £300 if you had bought it in Raven's Department Store," Hyacinth said, looking doubtfully at the cheque presented by this unprepossessing customer.

"Yes, I know and I think I'll wear it straight away if you wouldn't mind putting my other coat in a bag, please."

Hyacinth's face registered surprise as she read the label. "Luisa Spagnoli, we don't see many of these in here. Did you find it in one of the other charity shops?"

With all the dignity she could muster, Angharad replied, "No. I bought it in the Luisa Spagnoli shop in Florence!" Which prompted a sceptical look as the bag was handed over and her cheque placed in the till after further fiscal scrutiny.

It was, as she walked briskly away from the shop, that Angharad felt something hard in the hem of her coat knock uncomfortably against her leg, a coin caught in the lining perhaps. Back home, she investigated further. In one pocket, she found a slip of card with a phone number on it.

A section of stitching in the other pocket had been resewn firmly but clumsily by someone unaccustomed to working with a needle and thread. *How odd*, she thought, *that someone would mend a hole in a pocket without retrieving whatever had fallen through.* Carefully, she unpicked the stitching, retrieved the hard object from the lining and stared at it in astonishment.

It was a large, gold signet ring. Instead of a stone, an ornate, delicately crafted disc had been set into a heavy mount. An inscription had been roughly etched on the inside alongside an impressive row of unusual looking hallmarks. The gold disc was beautiful, but the ring itself was ugly and seemed strangely out of balance.

Ugly or not, the ring was obviously very valuable and ought to be returned to its rightful owner.

Next morning, Angharad went to a call box and dialled the telephone number she had found in the coat pocket. The phone rang twice followed by a click and silence. Finally, a recorded voice told her that the number was discontinued.

Reluctantly, she went back to re-engage with Hyacinth who was gearing up to advise her that charity shops did not operate a John Lewis-style returns policy, when she finally registered what Angharad had asked. No, she did not know who had handed in the coat.

"It was in a bag of clothes left in the doorway after hours in spite of the large sign telling people not to do that," said

Hyacinth, launching into a well-rehearsed sermon on the irresponsibility of people who abandoned donations outside the shop, prey to juvenile fire-raisers and thieves.

"Why do you want to know?" She asked impatiently.

Angharad hesitated before replying, "There was something, some…er…coins in the lining and I wanted to return them."

To her relief, two other customers entered the shop just at that moment. "Just put the coins in the donations box then," said Hyacinth over her shoulder as she swept towards the new arrivals. Angharad rattled a few coppers into the box and left the shop quickly wondering what to do next. The only link was the telephone number.

She knew from the prefix that it was an Edinburgh number. 'Discontinued' meant that at some point it had been live. What she needed was an Edinburgh phone book from two or three years ago. A helpful woman in the local library said they could access the current phone book for her, but doubted if they could get hold of an older one as these would probably have been pulped.

If Angharad could give her the year she was interested in, she would try to source a copy…Angharad thanked her and left. She would go to Edinburgh. She hadn't been to the city for years and she loved it.

It was madness. She had just spent twice as much as she could afford on a coat and now she was contemplating travelling 400 miles to solve a mystery based solely on a non-existent phone number. What did she hope the one-time owner of that phone number could tell her, assuming he or she was still alive and had simply changed contact details?

But by now her bag was packed and she was on her way to the bus station via the call box from which she had booked a bed in a city centre youth hostel for the following night.

The overnight bus from London to Edinburgh may have been cheap but it was an arduous journey made in the company of some boisterous students whose revelries finally subsided into enviable sleep at about three in the morning. Angharad emerged into the grey light of an Edinburgh dawn feeling stiff and exhausted.

Not so long ago she had flown business class, and stayed in four-star hotels. She had never imagined that one day she would travel in an overnight bus to a youth hostel she could barely afford.

Chapter 3
Rome, November
1993 to June 1994

For Angharad, a posting as First Secretary at the British Embassy in Rome had been a dream come true following the disappointment of an unsuccessful bid to become Head of Post at the Consulate General in Tallinn. She quickly discovered that Italians found her name, Angharad, difficult to pronounce, so to save embarrassment she abbreviated it to her childhood nickname Anya.

The job was challenging—trying to make sense of the mystifying twists and turns in Italy's labyrinthine political system was no easier than it had been in the days when Cicero threw down the gauntlet to Julius Caesar but, in compensation, Rome offered so many interesting possibilities outside work. Every street told part of Rome's millennial history.

In her mind's eye, Anya could see politicians in purple togas jostling merchants along the decumanus—the flagged road running through the centre of the Roman Forum; and a thousand years later, the hawkers, housewives and pickpockets thronging the narrow, cobbled alleyways of the historic centre.

However, history might judge Mussolini's vandalism of ancient spaces, the grandiose boulevards he created along the Imperial Forum and leading to St Peter's were certainly powerful statements. Buildings also had a story to tell.

Magnificent arches and columns dedicated to long-dead emperors and generals fought for space with ancient churches inside whose walls great artists like Michelangelo or Caravaggio had created glorious images more powerful than words. Elegant piazzas were adorned with breath-taking sculptures and fountains, and in summertime, tranquil courtyards filled with the sound of music and elegant little theatres showed quirky plays.

Anya had always enjoyed choral singing, loved making glorious music as part of something far greater than herself and she had managed to find a good choir to join on almost every one of her overseas postings. Apart from the chance to make music, it was also an excellent way of meeting interesting people beyond the confines of embassy circles.

Since her arrival in Rome two years earlier, she had sung with the prestigious *Coro Santa Cecilia* and had made friends with Farah Iravani, a Persian emigrée married to the Marchese Paladorata. One November evening after rehearsal, Farah announced that she was planning to hold a dinner party and very much wanted Anya to attend.

"There is a friend of ours, Amir Rashid, who has heard me talk about you and would like to meet you."

On the way to the car park, Anya couldn't resist asking, "And who exactly is this Amir Rashid and why on Earth would he want to meet me?"

"Amir is a consultant paediatric oncologist at the *Bambino Gesu* Hospital. Like me, he cannot go back to Iran. His father was a diplomat at the Persian Embassy in Rome at the time of the Shah but was immediately recalled in 1979 when the Shah fell and Ayatollah Khomeini returned from Paris."

"At that time, Amir had just finished post graduate medical school in Rome and decided to remain in Italy after a break to go travelling. I believe his father was imprisoned in Teheran for a number of years."

"None of which explains why a successful doctor in his forties—if my arithmetic is right—would want to meet a fifty year old British diplomat!"

"He is just tired of listening to me telling him how wonderful you are!"

"Farah, are you trying to match make?"

"Just come to dinner!"

On the way home, Anya couldn't help smiling to herself. Of course she would go to the dinner to please Farah, but there must be something seriously wrong if a successful consultant, constantly surrounded by attractive female colleagues, needed the services of a matchmaker to brighten up his social life! Perhaps he was gay and Farah was simply in denial; perhaps he had a string of women and Farah had decided it was time he settled down.

The following Friday, steeling herself for the worst, she joined Farah's other dinner party guests, covertly scanning the room for the unprepossessing man destined to be her partner for the evening. She almost spilled her drink in surprise as Farah approached accompanied by an incredibly handsome middle-aged man.

He was tall, with smooth, light brown skin and thick black hair cut short and streaked with silver. His handshake was firm and warm and his incredibly blue eyes—the legacy of some early Norse traveller—lit with gentle amusement as they looked directly into hers making her blush like a schoolgirl.

"I am delighted to meet you at last, Miss Wilson. Farah has been hiding you from me."

He must either be gay or have more women than he knows what to do with.

"It is a pleasure to meet you, Dr Rashid."

"Amir, please."

The rest of the evening passed in a happy haze and she was pleased when he suggested sharing a taxi home, accepting his assurance that he lived not far from her embassy flat in Trastevere. On the way, he asked if she liked opera and said he had tickets for a performance of *Der Rosenkavalier* in two weeks' time. Would she like to join him? She would.

After that, they met three or four times in December and then it was Christmas. Over dinner on the 23rd, Amir explained that he always worked Christmas Eve and Christmas Day to allow colleagues to spend time with their families, after which he would go to Cairo for a few days. Anya had already arranged to spend Christmas with friends in the Lake District.

Although, not particularly religious, she had always enjoyed the Christmas Eve Service in the ancient church at Ings, and looked forward to the brisk, chilly hill walks interspersed with long evenings chatting around the pub fire. She was strangely disappointed that Amir had made no mention of meeting on their return, but the disappointment was short-lived.

He phoned while freezing rain was dripping down her neck on a hill walk to Cartmel and informed her that it was 21 degrees and sunny in Cairo. Through chattering teeth, she said she was pleased for him.

"Would you like to thaw out in Florence for New Year?" He asked. "I could be there from 30 December until 2 January. Separate rooms, I promise—on my honour as a Persian gentleman."

At the Berchielli Hotel, they checked in to the promised separate rooms overlooking the River Arno and the picturesque Ponte Vecchio. Only one of the rooms would be regularly used. She discovered that Persian honour lasted no longer than the first lingering kiss at midnight in Piazza Santa Croce.

They saw a lot of each other in the following months and Anya tried not to question his occasional, unexplained absences. She wondered if there was someone else but knew she didn't have the courage to challenge him in case he ended the relationship. The first warning sign that she overlooked, occurred in early spring.

Amir told her he was going to a conference in Milan at the weekend. When Anya returned home on the Friday evening, she discovered a leak from the boiler and a pool of water gradually spreading across the kitchen floor.

There was no response from the maintenance team at the embassy and it took ages, fumbling through the phone book, to find an emergency plumber who told her to turn the water off and he would get to her whenever he could; he was on another lengthy job. She decided to phone Amir—not that he could do anything from Milan, but she needed to share the stress with someone.

His phone was switched off. He would be in conference or at dinner, of course, but it was still switched off at midnight and there had been no response to the messages she had left. The plumber had been and gone, but sleep evaded her, and she lay tossing and turning until falling into a troubled sleep as dawn was breaking.

Later that morning she phoned the hospital and asked if they could get a message to Amir at the conference. His department knew nothing about a conference. All they could tell her was that he was not due back at work until the following Monday. It was during that long weekend that she faced up to how little she really knew about him.

He didn't talk about his family other than to say they were in Iran and under constant surveillance. Did he have brothers or sisters? Had he ever been married? All he had admitted when asked was that he had one long, important relationship.

Why did a successful consultant not own his own home? Why was he sharing a rented flat with another doctor? Why had she never been invited there? All she knew was that he lived somewhere in the fashionable San Giorgio area.

Anya called Farah, but she could add very little to what Anya already knew. Amir was the darling of the Persian Emigré Community. As far as Farah was aware, he had never been married. His father had been a junior diplomat in Rome in the 50s, transferred to Paris in the 60s and was back as Head of Mission in Rome by 1970.

Amir had been educated in International Schools in Paris and Rome and had gone on to study medicine at Bologna University. She knew he often went abroad for lengthy periods—she presumed because of his international reputation in the treatment of childhood cancers. She tried to reassure Anya but she could hear the concern in her voice.

Perhaps he had forgotten the charger for his phone or had lost his phone. Perhaps the conference had nothing to do with his work. Perhaps...

His explanation was that there had been someone else. She was in Cairo and he had gone there to end the relationship. He said he should have done it sooner and that he was sorry he had lied to her. Why had she so readily and thankfully accepted such an unlikely explanation and apology?

There had been no more unexplained absences and Amir took her to Crete for a week in April in compensation. It was a glorious time of year. A profusion of wild orchids, purple anemones and delicate chamomile transformed the landscape into a riot of colour, breathing life into the ancient, golden stones of the island's hellenic past.

The sea had cast off its rough winter grey and, stretching as far as the eye could see, white tipped waves broke over the turquoise waters of early summer. Amir went for a run every morning, allowing Anya to indulge in an hour tucked up in bed reading about the places they would visit that day.

On his return, he would chase her out of bed pretending to grab her while dripping with sweat. Shrieking with laughter, they would end up in the shower together with the inevitable result that they seldom made it to breakfast.

There had been nothing to indicate that he did anything other than run for an hour, but an American out jogging at the same time would have noticed that on two mornings, Amir stopped at a bench overlooking the sea to talk briefly to a heavily-set man of Middle-Eastern appearance. Anya had noticed the American sitting at a table alone in the tiny restaurant they went to on the first night.

He had seemed strangely out of place—tall, muscular and with fair hair in the buzz cut typical of the American military. His pallor suggested that he was not in Crete to lie on beaches and his general demeanour did not suggest an underlying passion for Greek history and archaeology. Maybe he was on leave from deployment in the Middle East or the Balkans and simply liked Greek food or Greek women or Greek men.

She saw him again at the local supermarket later that week and thought nothing of it. She had no idea that her next encounter with him would be in Rome, or that it would be so terrifying.

By May, the spare room in Anya's apartment had filled up with Amir's belongings and he had substantially moved in without either of them formally admitting that this was the case. She knew the embassy rules about getting security clearance for anyone living with a member of staff in embassy property. So why had she not sought clearance?

Without admitting it to herself, she knew the reason. She knew permission would not have been granted. Early on in their relationship, she had taken Amir to a farewell drinks event at the Embassy Staff Club situated in the grounds of the main embassy building. Halfway through the evening, Amir had expressed a sudden interest in modern architecture.

They had left the club to walk through the grounds so that he could get a closer look at the iconic building designed by Basil Spence to replace the embassy destroyed by Israeli terrorists in 1946. They did not enter the building, but the following day, the head of security had appeared in Anya's office wanting to know why Amir had been seen wandering around the grounds the previous evening.

Anya had laughed off the concern, saying that Amir had probably been bored and had expressed an interest in modern architecture as a means of escape from a roomful of strangers. This had not convinced the head of security who asked what she knew about Amir and advised her to be very careful. He was far from convinced by Anya's assertion that Amir was a Persian emigré who had lived in Rome most of his life and was more Italian than the Italians.

"You could probably have called Ayatollah Khomeini a Persian emigré at one time," was his final comment as he left the office. He was worried. Something about Dr Rashid had set off alarm bells.

There had been a more serious incident in April when she had taken Amir to a concert at Villa Wolkonski, the British Ambassador's official residence in Rome. During the interval, Amir had been found on the first floor of the Residence claiming to be looking for a bathroom.

The security guard who had followed him up to the first floor had been fully aware that Amir's claim made no sense as he, personally, had shown Amir to the men's cloakroom on arrival. He did not question Amir further, but simply escorted him back to the ballroom where the second half of the concert was about to start, then called his superior. He had noted that Amir had not asked to return via the men's room, suggesting that his need had not been pressing.

The following morning, Anya found the head of security waiting for her as she arrived at the embassy. Without preamble, he had asked her what Amir had been doing at the villa the night before. Although, Anya knew that Amir ought to have known exactly where the bathrooms were, she dismissed the suggestion that he had been prompted by anything other than idle curiosity.

"I think you are being rather too trusting of your friend's intentions and I am formally advising you not to bring Dr Rashid onto embassy property again. I would also advise you to end the relationship as I am very sure Dr Rashid is not all that he seems to be."

Anya was furious. She felt patronised by the man's manner and angry at the slur on Amir's character. If something in what he said touched on unspoken doubts in her own mind, she immediately suppressed the thought. Besides, the head of security had been unable to produce any evidence to back his insinuations. Anya, therefore, chose to ignore the warning and, far from ending the relationship, had allowed Amir to move into her apartment.

One evening towards the end of May, Amir had arrived home late and exhausted. It had been a long, dispiriting day with serious complications arising in surgery on a four year old with a malignant brain tumour. He didn't know whether she would make it; the next forty-eight hours would tell.

To make matters worse, a little boy he had been treating over the last two years had unexpectedly died of heart failure that afternoon. He had left his laptop in the hospital by mistake and needed to print off the notes for a presentation he was due to make the following day in Milan. He asked if he could use Anya's computer. He would get a colleague at the hospital to forward the document by email.

"Milan again!" She said.

"Genuine, this time," he replied with a sheepish smile. "You can check for yourself, if you just let me print

44

everything off here, otherwise I'll have to go back to the hospital."

"My laptop is on the dining room table," she called from the kitchen where she was preparing dinner.

"Can you enter the password for me," he called from the dining room.

"My hands are covered in onion and tomato just now, it's frg39iK224."

In the short time it took her to assemble the meal, he had managed to print the conference documents. She did not know that he had also sent a coded email to 'a person of interest' in Cairo, nor that the CIA had the email traffic to the Cairo address under surveillance.

Trastevere, June 1994

The first Sunday in June was a glorious day. They rose early and had a lazy breakfast on the terrace before heading out for a walk up the hill on the other side of the river to Santa Sabina, stopping to admire the Circus Maximus on the way. Sun gilded the stones of Septimius Severus's Palace standing sentinel as it had for almost two millennia over the green sweep of the arena below.

At the top of the Sabine hill, they gazed out over the panorama of Rome, pointing out famous buildings and trying to identify their own apartment amid the jumble of terracotta roofs across the river in Trastevere.

They had a late lunch at their favourite trattoria, lingering over coffee and a delicious Amaretto to watch the passeggiata—a ritual for Roman families with grandparents and children, babes in arms, dogs, prams and wheelchairs all out to enjoy the late afternoon sunshine and walk off the effects of Sunday lunch.

Back at the apartment, they started to plan an autumn holiday in Cyprus. They didn't want to go on an organised tour but had collected several travel guides for inspiration and these lay spread out over the dining room table while they discussed ideas and began to plan their itinerary. As the light faded, Amir got up and went to the kitchen returning with two large glasses of the soft red wine of the Roman hills.

"We should take these out onto the terrace, the view tonight is fantastic," he said.

It was true. The low evening sun had bathed the rooftops in fiery reds and the river beyond shone like a mirror. They drank the wine and kissed, slowly and passionately before tumbling into bed, holiday planning temporarily suspended.

The following morning, Amir rose very early. He had a long surgical list that day and needed time to prepare. He brought Anya tea before he left saying that he should be back by seven that evening.

"We can finish planning our holiday after dinner," he said as he left, popping his head round the bedroom door once again to add, "provided you can desist from distracting me the way you did last night!"

The cushion she threw missed its target and hit the closing door. The last thing she heard was his laughter as he headed for the lift.

Chapter 4
The Nightmare Begins,
June 1994

Cell phones were not allowed in the embassy, so it was not until six pm when she retrieved her phone from the security desk that Anya noticed that Amir had left a voicemail.

"Caris..."—his voice?—followed by another issuing a brief, harsh command. Suddenly and irrationally, she felt fear. She tried to return the call and an automated message told her that the number could not be reached and she should try again later. She did, every half hour until nine when the automated voice informed her that the number was no longer active.

She tried to control rising panic telling herself that he was probably still in theatre—after all, it only took unexpected complications in one operation to put the whole day's surgical list back. Maybe his phone had been stolen by one of the many migrants wandering the streets of Rome and those were the voices she had heard. But why would thieves have called her number?

And Anya was sure the second voice had spoken in Farsi—by then she recognised its cadences even if she didn't understand what was said. Reluctantly, she had to concede that kleptomaniac Iranians were not a prominent constituent of Rome's criminal underworld. Try as she might to convince herself that nothing sinister had happened to Amir, normal explanations for his disappearance simply did not add up.

Finally, she called the hospital and spoke to a worried young doctor. Dr Rashid had left the hospital suddenly at four pm in the company of two foreign men. He had just come out of theatre and it was unheard of for him to leave the hospital until he had checked his patients in the recovery room, or to leave the registrar to carry out the final operation of the day without any warning.

They did not know where Dr Rashid was and he wasn't answering his telephone. That much Anya already knew.

"What did the men look like?"

"I was still in theatre, it was a nurse who saw them. She said they were waiting in the corridor and she initially thought they must be relatives of a patient. She said they were rough-looking, dark-skinned men and didn't look like the sort of people Dr Rashid would normally associate with. One of them took Dr Rashid's arm as soon as he left the theatre and the three of them disappeared down the corridor."

"He left in his surgical scrubs without picking up his jacket or his briefcase. We called his home but he isn't there and we are very worried."

Called his home? There had been no call to the flat but, of course, his home address as far as hospital records were concerned was a rented flat somewhere in San Giorgio.

"Has anyone contacted the police?"

"Not yet, the hospital director says we should wait till tomorrow morning and call then if he doesn't turn up. The director thinks that the most likely explanation is that he was called away on an urgent personal matter, and as there was no sign of a struggle or coercion, it should be assumed that he left voluntarily."

Midnight came and went and with it fitful, terror-filled sleep: Amir thrown into the back of a truck and driven away; trying to run after him on legs that wouldn't move; Amir captured by criminals and forced to remove organs from children (triggered by a TV documentary on people trafficking and the organ transplant racket in North Africa).

She awoke utterly exhausted and with an overwhelming sense of desolation, sent an email to the embassy to say she wouldn't be in and called the hospital. Dr Rashid had not appeared and had not made contact. She buried her head in her hands, hot tears rolling unbidden down her cheeks. Wearily getting to her feet, she went into the spare room and searched through Amir's belongings looking for anything that might explain his disappearance.

She found his official address in Via dei Fienili on a discarded envelope from the *Ospedale Pediatrico Bambino Gesu* and on impulse decided to go there. Someone had shared that flat with him and that someone might know where he was. The building didn't take long to find. It was an imposing, four floor apartment building with a pillared entrance.

A polished brass panel displayed the names of its occupants, typically two surnames per household as is common in Italy. Anya's head swam as she read the names of the occupants of the third floor apartment: *Akhtar. Rashid.* Summoning all the courage she could muster, she rang the bell. There was no response.

Stepping back, she looked up at the windows on the third floor. Was it just her imagination, or had she seen a fleeting movement behind one of them? She had walked a few steps along the street, unsure what to do next when she saw the door of the building open and an elderly man stepping out. She called to him and asked if he could let her into the building.

"The bell to my friend's apartment doesn't appear to be working," she explained with what she hoped was a reassuring smile.

After a moment's hesitation, the man took out his key and let her into the hallway. A modern lift stood in the well of a broad marble stairway. Instinctively, she took the stairs, wishing to avoid the noise made by a lift. Reaching the third floor she stopped briefly to catch her breath before approaching a highly polished mahogany door.

She rang the bell. No response. She rang it again. Still no response. She struck the brass door knocker as hard as she could against the door. No response, but she was sure she heard movement and the cover of the spy hole being moved aside. She knocked again.

This time she heard a chain being drawn across and the door opened a fraction to reveal a thin woman in her late fifties, wisps of grey hair emerging from a dark-coloured hijab and fear written all over her face. Anya also noticed two suitcases standing at the door.

"Who are you?" The woman asked in an urgent whisper.

"I'm a friend of Amir's and he's disapp…"

The woman cut her short. "He's not here, I don't know where he is and I don't want to know!"

The door closed abruptly almost hitting Anya in the face. Was the woman telling the truth? Was Amir hiding somewhere in the apartment? Why was the woman so afraid? Defeated, Anya left the building and had almost reached the end of the street when she saw a limousine with darkened windows draw up outside the entrance to Amir's building.

Two men of Middle Eastern appearance got out, one talking into a phone held against his ear. A few minutes later, the main door opened and Dr Akhtar stepped out and handed her cases to one of the men before climbing into the back seat of the car. Anya stood transfixed to the spot; two people with the same address, two abrupt departures involving dark-skinned men and no sign of a struggle or coercion. Could it possibly be a coincidence?

As the car pulled away, Dr Soraya Akhtar, internationally acclaimed industrial chemist and undercover spy on behalf of the Islamic Republic of Iran, saw the woman standing at the end of the street—the woman who was the cause of this crisis. Tense with pent up anger and fear, she silently cursed Amir.

She had had to be pulled from vitally important industrial espionage because that idiot had attracted the attention of the CIA by getting himself involved with a British diplomat, confirming all she had ever suspected about the fecklessness of beautiful men. As a result, it hadn't taken long for the CIA to turn its searchlights onto her.

She had seen the American jogging along her street—no one went jogging along Via dei Fienili unless they had some ulterior motive; and she had also seen him jogging alongside the perimeter fence surrounding the petro-chemical research facility where she worked.

She knew the type and was afraid, very afraid of capture by the Americans because, unlike Amir, she was no ordinary spy and she was all too aware of the fate Americans reserved for captured enemy assets! She would not feel safe until her afternoon flight touched down in Teheran.

Anya spent the rest of the day in a daze, wandering through the streets of Rome until darkness fell. She couldn't face going home to an empty apartment, so she phoned Farah who was in Turin with her husband and couldn't talk for long. In the end, she sat alone among the crowds by the Pantheon, staring into space, leaving others to marvel at the magnificent temple financed by one of Ancient Rome's most famous generals.

Back home, she found several messages from the embassy on her phone, but none from Amir. She felt hungry but couldn't face eating, so she took the half bottle of wine left over from Sunday night out onto the terrace and tried to make sense of the events of the past few days.

Two things she was sure of: when Amir had left on Monday morning he had no idea that he wouldn't be returning that evening; and Amir would never voluntarily walk out on his patients and colleagues. The rest made no sense at all.

The following morning, she was roused from troubled sleep by an insistent ringing of the doorbell. Groggily, she looked at her watch. It was seven-thirty. "Amir without his keys!" She rushed to the door and looked at the face on the security screen. It wasn't Amir, it was Andrew Blyth, the head of security at the embassy with another man.

"Andrew, it's half past seven in the morning. What are you doing here?"

"I'm afraid this can't wait, Anya, you need to let us in."

Reluctantly, she released the entrance door, pulled on a dressing gown and stood in the doorway to the apartment until Andrew and his colleague reached the top of the stairs.

"You must come with us now, Anya. There has been a serious breach of security and it involves you."

She stared at Andrew in disbelief. "What breach of security and why does it involve me?"

"I can't say any more at the moment. We were looking for you all day yesterday. You must come with us now and we can discuss the detail once we get to the embassy."

She felt as though the world as she knew it had suddenly turned on its head.

With a sudden burst of defiance, she said, "I am not going anywhere until I have showered, dressed and had a coffee."

Andrew looked nonplussed. "I am not supposed to let you out of my sight."

"If you think I will let you anywhere near my bathroom or bedroom, you will need to think again. Besides, I am hardly likely to jump out of a window four floors above street level."

"You will need to give me your phone and laptop first."

She threw the phone at him. It caught him on the chest before landing on the floor at his feet. "And the laptop is on the table right in front of you! Help yourself. Anything else you need, just ask."

Andrew looked as if he wished he were anywhere else but there.

She was taken to a small room at the embassy. A man she vaguely recognised stood as she entered and introduced himself as Jed Baker from the US Embassy. He was tall with a blonde military-style brush cut—the American she had seen in Crete! He had CIA written all over him.

Christopher Nutall, Deputy Head of Mission at the embassy, broke in, visibly annoyed by Baker's arrogant dismissal of protocol, and stated firmly that he would conduct the interview. Mr Baker was there simply 'as a courtesy to our American friends'. That was not how it worked out.

"Miss Wilson, we have a number of serious questions we would like to put to you," Baker began without permission or preamble.

"I can't think of anything I know that could possibly be of interest to 'our American friends' as Christopher calls you."

"I am afraid I must disagree with you on that point. First of all, you are in a relationship with someone of considerable interest to us. Are you aware of the real identity of Amir Rashid?"

Anya stared at him, defiance slowly draining from her. "What do you mean by 'real identity'?"

"Did you know that he works for VAJA, the Iranian Intelligence Service?"

"Don't be ridiculous. Amir is *persona non grata* as far as the Iranian regime is concerned. He has Italian citizenship and is a respected consultant who has worked at Rome's best known children's hospital for years. He and his family were staunch supporters of the Shah."

"I think you'll find that that is not the case. His father provided covert support for Ayatollah Khomeini during his exile and remains close to the present regime, even in retirement."

She felt the room dissolve around her; Baker's voice just white noise as his questions came thick and fast, each one hitting with relentless force.

"Do you know who alerted the Iranians to the fact that Rashid's cover was blown, giving them time to recall him before we could question him?"

"Are you accusing me? I have no idea what you are talking about."

"Did you not ask yourself why a man who could have had any woman he wanted, chose to form a relationship with you?"

She let the implied insult pass. Christopher looked extremely embarrassed.

"Knowing he was a national of a hostile state, why did you simply accept his cover story without carrying out due diligence?"

"What due diligence was necessary? I knew where he worked, I knew what he did. The staff at the *Bambino Gesu* have known and worked with him for almost twenty years. The Persian Emigré Community knows him well. Consultant oncologists don't have the time or the inclination to spy if that is what you are accusing him of."

"You may be surprised to learn that all sorts of people find the time and inclination to spy; the more unlikely the public role, the better for the sponsoring agency. Did you not question where he went and what he did on his frequent absences from Rome?"

"A few dinner dates in the early months did not confer the right to subject him to the third degree about what he did at other times. Recently, there have been no unexplained absences."

"Are you aware that he has a wife and two children in Teheran?"

She didn't hear the rest of the questions which would, in any case, be repeated endlessly over the next few days. The news of a wife and children was so devastating that her mind went completely blank. The questioning went on. If she answered, she had no recollection later of what she said.

"Why did you bring him onto embassy property in spite of warnings from security?"

"Why did you continue the relationship in spite of being told to end it?"

"Why did you allow him to live in an embassy apartment without proper clearance—clearance you must have known would never be given?"

"Why did you give him access to your embassy laptop and password?"

"Did you discuss UK policy on Iran with him—policy regarding Iran's support for Hezbollah for example, or UK's stance on international sanctions, or the UK Government's intentions in the region following Iraq's failed invasion of Kuwait…"

Christopher interrupted the torrent of questions, irritated beyond endurance by Baker's arrogance. "The Middle East is not Miss Wilson area of expertise. You would do well to confine your questioning to the matter in hand."

Baker carried on regardless.

"You received a phone message from Dr Rashid on the day he left. Was the first word a coded message?"

"The first word?" Anya asked, jolted back to the present.

"Cari."

"It would be the beginning of Carissima, it's what he called me, but the message was cut short."

Baker looked confused.

"It means darling," Christopher said with more than a hint of malice directed at the American.

Ignoring Christopher's response, Baker continued his relentless questioning, "Another man spoke on the phone. Who was he? What did he say?"

"I don't know who the voice belonged to—I didn't understand what he said—I don't understand any of this."

Christopher intervened again, "It was Farsi for *give me that phone!* I checked with our people."

Anya was confined to a safe house that night and the following night. By day, questions, endless questions rained down on her and at night, in solitude, other questions of love and betrayal tormented her. Finally she was released, suspended from duty with immediate effect and put on a flight to London.

Her personal belongings would be forwarded to her. She would face further investigation in London.

Chapter 5
Amir Rashid

Kamran Teherani watched in relief as the plane took off from Fiumicino Airport bound for Imam Khomeini Airport in Teheran. "I should have put that idiot on a plane years ago," he said to himself—'would have done if he hadn't been his father's son'. He might be his father's son, but he wasn't the man Reza Rashid had been.

His father had provided invaluable information to Ayatollah Ruhollah Khomeini throughout the latter's exile while maintaining his cover as the Shah's man in Paris and Rome.

It had been Reza Rashid's idea that Amir should remain in Rome as a 'sleeper' after a period of training in Iran, during which time he had entered into an arranged marriage with the daughter of powerful family friends and fathered twin girls.

The absence of two years between medical school and becoming a junior doctor at the *Bambino Gesu* had been explained away as 'travelling', a popular pursuit among wealthy young Europeans anxious to postpone the realities of earning a living for as long as possible.

He had gone to Australia on his Italian passport for two months during that time so that he had more than textbook knowledge to fall back on should conversations veer onto the dangerous ground of what he had done while travelling. Kamran had been his 'minder' since 1983 and he had often wondered how strongly Amir really identified with Iran—a country in which he had spent so little time.

He had been born in Rome, attended schools in Paris and Rome and medical school in Bologna. Iran had been where he had spent holidays with his grandparents, and brief spells with a wife he didn't love and children he hardly knew. Iran was a foreign country to Amir who was, to all intents and purposes, Italian.

Amir had quickly become the darling of the emigré community in Rome and in the early 80s when Khomeini's grip on power was far from secure, he had picked up some useful information about the activities of the Shah's supporters in Rome. However, the fading dreams of elderly emigrés had long since ceased to pose a serious threat to the security of Iran.

The real danger lay in the actions of hostile states, the USA, Britain, Israel and Saudi to name but a few. Italy was not a hostile state and Amir's deployment in Rome was about to be terminated when he made friends with a prominent emigrée, Farah Iravani, Marchesa Paladorata. Not that Farah Iravani posed any threat to the security of the Islamic Republic of Iran.

She would not have welcomed the opportunity to abandon the freedom of her glamorous lifestyle in Rome to return to Teheran, Shah or no Shah. Her husband, Giovanni di Melo, Marchese Paladorata, on the other hand, was of great interest. He was executive director of one of Italy's largest petro-chemical companies and a man of international influence in his field.

However, it had soon become clear that the Marchese was not in the habit of dropping gems of information about international dealings in the petro-chemical industry over dinner with the charismatic doctor who amused his wife. It was the brilliant industrial chemist Soraya Akhtar who had proved to be a source of important information from that sector. Amir's usefulness in Rome had expired.

In October 1993, Kamran had told Amir that he should settle his affairs in Rome and await arrangements for recall to Iran. If all he was good at was saving the lives of sick children, he could do that to greater national benefit in Teheran without the additional costs and risks of keeping him in Rome. That was when Amir had dropped an unexpected bombshell. He had met and formed a relationship with a First Secretary at the British Embassy.

Kamran now regretted his decision to hold off to find out what that relationship might yield. It had yielded nothing. At a meeting in Cairo in March 1994, Amir had told Kamran he had access to the British Embassy and to the Ambassador's Residence at the Villa Wolkonsky, and had carried out reconnaissance at both sites. The man was hopeless! What use did he imagine a plan of embassy buildings would have been?

The Iranian Government already knew the layout of both and was not in any case planning to occupy either, take hostages or plant a bomb. Besides which, it was unlikely that embassy staff would leave confidential papers lying around waiting to be photographed by Amir. To add to Kamran's headaches, in March, Amir's influential wife had travelled to Cairo to join her husband and Amir had asked for a divorce.

He later assured Kamran that it was because he and his wife had drifted apart, not because he had fallen in love with Anya Wilson. Kamran had not been convinced.

At what point had Amir attracted the attention of the CIA? That was something Kamran had missed and for which he would doubtless be held to account. He would have been surprised to learn that it had been a few years earlier when Amir was treating the son of a US army captain based at Camp Derby near Pisa.

The boy had a rare form of leukaemia and so contact with the family had continued over a period of time. The captain had become suspicious when Amir started asking questions about US military bases in Italy and had reported his concern to his superiors.

With nothing useful coming from Amir, Kamran had insisted on meeting at the end of April.

"Not in Cairo," had been the reply. "Another unexplained trip to Cairo would make Anya suspicious. If you can't come to Rome, it will need to be while we are on holiday in Crete."

In Crete, Amir had assured Kamran that he had moved in with Anya and would soon have access to her work laptop. In the end, all Kamran got was a coded message saying that Amir had access to the embassy IT system. Kamran didn't know that the CIA had the email address Amir had used to contact him under surveillance and had traced the origin of Amir's email to a British Embassy computer.

It had been Kamran's contact inside the American Embassy who had alerted him to the fact that both Amir and Soraya Akhtar were being watched. The CIA was particularly concerned about Amir's relationship with a British diplomat.

He had had to get Amir and Soraya out fast before the whole thing developed into an international diplomatic fracas.

In the end, getting Amir and Soraya out of Rome before the CIA moved against them had been touch and go. He wondered with a certain grim satisfaction what was going to be worse for Amir—his debriefing at the Ministry of Intelligence or his debriefing by his wife's family. Either way, Kamran was finally relieved of an increasingly unreliable and unmanageable 'asset'.

Amir stared unseeingly out of the aircraft window, utterly traumatised by events of the last twenty-four hours and by thoughts of the devastation he had left in his wake.

His mind was in turmoil, nightmare imaginings appeared and disappeared, became confused, setting his nerves on edge; images of desperate parents learning that their child's surgery was to be postponed; his senior registrar struggling to cope with an impossible workload; the distress of colleagues left inexplicably leaderless. Worst of all were the images of Anya. Why had he not been honest with her?

But how could he have told her the truth? He would have lost her when she learned that he was not an emigré but working for the Iranian regime: that his initial motivation had been to use her to betray her country; that he was already married and had two children in Iran. Now she would be learning all of this in the worst possible way, under interrogation.

She would never know how quickly and absolutely he had come to love her; never know that he had asked for a divorce; never know that he would not have betrayed her even if he had found plans for a full-scale invasion of Iran on her dining room table; never know that he had come to the end of delaying tactics and would be forced to return to Iran; never know that he had been applying to emigrate to Australia, in the hope that his minders would lose track of him and that she could join him there.

The CIA would have found the partially completed application form on his desk where he had left it, uncertain how to complete the section on marital status and dependents. They would tell her about the application and that her name did not appear on it to ensure that her sense of betrayal was complete.

They would hope that disillusionment would finally turn to anger and she would tell them all she knew about agent Rashid. He didn't care what happened to him now, he had already lost everything that mattered. He felt sick at the thought of what was probably happening to her at that very moment and he was consumed by guilt at the devastation his intrusion in her life had inflicted on her.

Chapter 6
Berlin, 1945

Hanna Brandt collapsed onto the hard chair in a small, cluttered office at the end of a Nightingale ward and buried her head in her hands. She was beyond exhaustion. She had been on duty for eighteen hours trying to do her best for the relentless flow of severely injured and traumatised young men arriving at the Königin Elisabeth Krankenhaus (Queen Elisabeth Hospital) in Berlin.

By 1945, the once prestigious hospital lacked everything from medical staff to dressings, clean sheets and medication. Makeshift beds crowded every available space in corridors and landings and the few doctors and nurses left could do little to alleviate the suffering. An all-pervading smell of industrial disinfectant only added to other heavy odours of unwashed men, sickness and infection.

Worst of all was the lack of morphine, most of which had been redirected to the High Command, no doubt to assuage top-ranking officials' night-time terrors at having wrought such devastation on Germany.

It had been so different during her two years in medical school immediately before the war. In those days, hospitals had been fully staffed, well-equipped and there had been an overriding sense of optimism and purpose. During her third year, she had abandoned her studies—temporarily she thought—to help the war effort by enrolling as a nurse, never imagining that the war would grind on for six grim years.

Now she was in sole charge of wards and corridors full of men injured in the last desperate attempt to save Berlin from the advancing Russians. She hadn't been back to her small flat in Heinrich Roller Strasse near Alexanderplatz for more than a week now. It took too long to walk, her bike had been stolen and there was no fuel for public transport. The sound of heavy shelling came closer every day.

At first, the thought of the advancing Russians had terrified her—rumours of their brutal treatment of civilian populations were rife. But now she felt too tired to care. All she wanted was for the terrifying noises of war and the screams of injured men to stop so that she could sleep.

An orderly interrupted her brief rest to tell her that a new wave of wounded men had arrived and were lying on the floor at what had once been the reception area. He wanted to know what he should do with them. Slowly with aching limbs and a pounding head, Hanna got to her feet and followed the orderly out.

She had almost finished checking the new arrivals, angry as ever that there was so little she could do for them, when she let out a gasp as she knelt beside a painfully thin young man with flesh wounds on his right cheek and shoulder, his whole body shaking in shock.

"Hans Dietrich," she whispered. "It's Hanna, Hanna Brandt. We were at Heidelberg together, do you remember?"

"H...Hanna! I can hardly believe it!" He replied, clutching her hand tightly as his body convulsed. "I am so cold...Where am I? Are you all right?"

"Shh...You are in the Königen Elisabeth Hospital. I'll try to find you a blanket."

She had seen it all too often—physical wounds which were not particularly serious as long as infection didn't set in, but severe mental trauma for which no treatment was available in war-torn Berlin.

Hanna and Hans Dietrich von Seidel had been good friends at medical school and in the summer of 1939, she and three other companions had joined him at Schloss Stauffensee, Hans Dietrich's family home. The castle was decidedly kitsch and Hans Dietrich had joked that his father's inspiration in enlarging the original villa had been the palaces of the mad King Ludwig of Bavaria.

Hanna had found his father and older brother, Hans Peter, cold and intimidating, but she had liked his sister, Stefania, and simply adored his rather lost little brother, Hans Albrecht. The adoration had been reciprocal, and Hans Albrecht had appointed himself as faithful guide and companion to this pretty, affectionate lady who had suddenly brightened his rather lonely young life.

That summer belonged to a different world. Hitler had already begun 'to make Germany great again' by annexing the Sudetenland and had made no secret of his intentions regarding Germany's right to 'the grain baskets of Ukraine', but they had been young and had no idea of where this expansionism would lead.

That summer, they had played tennis and spent languid hours soaking up the sun around the pool. They had enjoyed long walks through forests and along lakesides, and lively evenings in beer gardens. Hans Dietrich had left university to join the Wehrmacht in 1940 and she hadn't seen him since.

The sound of Russian artillery bombardment was coming ever closer and the order came to evacuate the hospital a few days after Hans Dietrich arrived. Hanna was desperate. Few of her patients were fit to be transferred and there were no places for them in other hospitals anyway.

Few of the walking wounded had any homes to go to or people to care for them, but as the shells began to explode around the hospital, there was no alternative. Tears rolled down her cheeks as she watched a heart-breaking stream of patients wend westwards on wheelchairs, stretchers, crutches or packed onto the few trucks they had been able to commandeer.

Ambulances were a forgotten dream. She decided to take Hans Dietrich to her flat in Heinrich Roller Strasse then return to the hospital to remain with the few patients who could not be moved.

The 11 kilometre walk was an ordeal for Hans Dietrich. They took side streets to avoid loud traffic noises which caused him to panic. Although, his wounds were not particularly serious, he had lost a lot of blood and they had to stop frequently so that he could rest. Several times Hanna had to cajole him to get back on his feet.

At a crossroads, they saw one of the military patrols rounding up every male with the strength to wield a weapon and Hanna had to push a terrified Hans Dietrich into a derelict garden until the patrol disappeared with its pitiful band of old men and children. Once she was sure that the coast was clear, she had returned to the garden but there was no sign of Hans Dietrich.

She scanned the mounds of broken masonry and overgrown bushes, but he was nowhere to be seen. Gingerly, she walked along a rubble-strewn path towards the bombed-out house, checking for signs of unexploded munitions amongst the accumulated rubbish. Berliners had learned to be careful.

The ground floor windows had been blown out but the imposing front door remained defiantly intact, the securely locked but poignantly redundant defender of a once imposing home. Looking through a window frame, she saw Hans Dietrich curled up in a far corner of the devastated room. He was moaning and shaking uncontrollably.

Hanna called to him but he did not react. She called again, urgently this time, encouraging him to get up, telling him they would soon be safely home.

"Just leave me," he whispered. "They will find me anyway and I'll only put you at risk."

It took almost an hour of increasingly desperate pleading and cajoling to get Hans Dietrich back onto his feet and on the move again. They finally reached her flat without further incident and she put Hans Dietrich into her bed to rest. She barely had time to explain that she would have to return to the hospital before he fell asleep.

There was almost nothing to eat in the house, but she put a tin of sausages she had been saving for a special occasion along with some hard biscuits on the table with a note telling him to help himself.

On her way back to the hospital, she worried about how she was going to feed both of them on her meagre rations.

There was no question of informing the authorities that she had a sick man living with her, they were rounding up men in a worse state than Hans Dietrich for the final, pointless stand against the Russians.

She had nothing to exchange for goods on the black market and the last of the stores in the hospital kitchen had left with the evacuees that morning.

An old orderly and a nurse had moved the remaining patients into one wing of the hospital. Three men had died while Hanna had been away and, without food, equipment and medication, the others were unlikely to survive much longer. Against the odds, a few would survive long enough to be thrown out to certain death by the invading Russians.

Her overriding preoccupation was how to find food for Hans Dietrich. Long before the war, the Königen Elisabeth Krankenhaus had been a famous children's hospital and until the early 40s, a small children's department had continued to operate from a villa in the grounds. It would have had a separate kitchen!

Among the vast array of keys abandoned in the janitor's office, Hanna found a set that belonged to the villa. As darkness was falling, she left the eerily empty main hospital heading for the villa. She had taken a nurse's night-time torch with her as even if the lights in the villa still worked, she did not want to draw attention to what she was doing.

It didn't take long to find the kitchen, but the shelves and cupboards were bare of everything apart from a few pans and cooking utensils. Discouraged, she was about to leave the kitchen when she noticed a passage leading to the back door. In the passageway, she found a locked door and after several failed attempts, found the right key.

Inside there were several tins of dried milk, two packets of rusks for teething babies, half-empty sacks of dried beans and lentils, a few tins of vegetables and, an unimaginable luxury, a tin of salt butter. The problem was how to get this wonderful horde home. Anyone carrying a large bag was liable to be robbed or stopped by the police.

Anyone the police or militia found with a supply of food most Berliners could only dream of would be arrested as a black marketeer. The Russians would have arrived before she could carry much of it away as she would be able to conceal only a few items at a time on the long walk back to her apartment.

That was when she remembered the battered pram she had seen in the entrance vestibule. She ran back along the main corridor to check it out. One of the wheels was wobbly but it pushed along quite well if in a slightly drunken fashion. Wonderfully, it had a compartment in the base of the chassis for holding shopping and baby necessities.

Quickly, she filled the base of the pram with as much as it would hold and slid the cover over. She had been tempted to fill the main body of the pram as well but knew that would be disastrous if she were stopped and searched. She also knew that a woman pushing an apparently empty pram would arouse suspicion and she searched the rest of the villa for what she needed—a lifelike doll.

The only large doll she found among piles of abandoned toys had lost an eye and one of her legs but, swaddled in a blanket, she hoped it might just pass casual observation. She would be a nurse pushing a sick baby away from the advancing Russian army.

Hanna locked the pram and its precious contents in the store cupboard overnight. A curfew had been in place since February and although emergency services were exempt, she had no official authorisation for being on the streets between eight at night and five am. Besides, nowhere was safe at night-time when the allied bombers arrived to pulverise what little of the once fine city was left standing.

Back in the main hospital, Hanna told her two colleagues to get some rest. She would call them if she needed help overnight. For a long time, she held the hand of a young boy who was crying softly for his mother.

He was no more than fourteen or fifteen and she was filled with impotent anger at a nation which had allowed a madman to drag it to the gates of hell over the bodies of its children. There was nothing more she could do for the boy as fever raged unchecked through his thin body. Nothing apart from allowing him to believe she was his mother and at his side.

Morning eventually came and Hanna handed over to the other nurse, promising that she would rest for a while and be back by late afternoon. Instead, she made her way to the villa, retrieved the pram and pushed it out of the back door. There was a gate leading onto a lane behind the villa and Hanna made for that to avoid being seen from the hospital.

Inevitably, the gate was locked and it took Hanna a while to find the right key and even longer to get the stiff lock to turn.

Negotiating a pram along bomb-damaged streets, not least a heavily laden pram with a wobbly wheel was no easy matter and progress was heart-stoppingly slow. Patrols were out everywhere and long queues of starving people blocked the pavements outside bakers' shops, but nobody stopped her.

Not far from her flat, the wobbly wheel finally parted company from the pram, making the last part of the journey a nightmare of aching arms and shoulders as she sought to keep the pram stable on three wheels.

Once inside the apartment block, she propped the pram up under the stair well and began the slow process of taking the items one at a time from the base, wrapping them in the doll's blanket and carrying them up to the flat, terrified that a neighbour might appear at any moment and ask what she was carrying.

She found Hans Dietrich sitting on a chair by the bedroom window staring into space. He turned round slowly when he heard her voice and gave her a wan smile as he rose unsteadily to his feet.

"Thank you so much for helping me, but I should leave now. It is too risky for you to have me here."

"Come through to the living room and let's talk about it."

As they entered the living room, Hanna noticed that Hans Dietrich had left half of the sausage and biscuits she had laid on the table for him earlier. He had left them for her.

"I'm not sure there is much to talk about," said Hans Dietrich as he pulled a chair out for Hanna and she smiled wistfully at this rare gesture of pre-war etiquette. "As far as the army is concerned, I am probably classed as a deserter by now. Men much more seriously injured than I am have been sent back to the front."

"Dietrich," she said gently, "you also have shell shock. It will be many months before the waves of involuntary shaking lessen sufficiently for you to be able to take up arms again even if you want to. Shell shock is far more debilitating than almost any other non-fatal injury. I've seen it far too often.

Your unit was wiped out and who knows where the rest of the army is by now."

"Hitler and his crew of warmongering criminals are safely tucked up in a bunker. Here is as safe as anywhere right now as long as you are careful not to be seen."

"I would put you at enormous risk by staying here and I cannot allow that. Perhaps I could lie low for a while at that ruined house where we hid yesterday. Just until I can control the shaking."

"Dietrich, apart from everything else, that house is being used by squatters. I saw old blankets, cups and food wrappers in all the ground floor rooms while I was looking for you and the place stinks of urine. I will not be at any more risk than anyone else in this city provided no one knows you are here. The days when friends and neighbours called are long gone."

Somewhere nearby a siren went off and Hanna watched helplessly as Hans Dietrich struggled to control the violent tremors wracking his body.

"Why don't you lie down for a while and I'll make something for us to eat before I go back to the hospital. We still have twenty-three patients who are too badly injured to move. I just hope the Russians leave them in peace." As Hanna said that, she caught the look of bitter compassion in Hans Dietrich's eyes. Both knew the likely fate of badly injured Germans who found themselves at the mercy of Russian troops.

While Hans Dietrich slept, Hanna washed his uniform as best she could with a precious sliver of soap and cold water. *At least,* she thought, *if his clothes were wet, he couldn't slip out while she was at the hospital.* She laid his Iron Cross carefully on the table, hoping that it would remind him of the courage he had already shown in the service of his country. Hoping that it would lessen the guilt he clearly felt at his present weakened state.

Hanna had learned something of his war during the few days he had spent at the hospital—two years of desert warfare with the Afrika Korps under Rommel then, following the capitulation of Italy in September 1943, the Italian campaign. The Italian campaign which had started as a harsh lesson to a former ally had ended as a bitterly fought retreat before the relentless advance of allied forces, Hitler's demented rant of 'No retreat!' ringing in his soldiers' ears.

He had told her how all through the freezing winter of 1944, he and his men had tried to hold the Gothic line against advancing units of the allied army and against the unpredictable and increasingly audacious attacks by Italian partisans—men and women who knew the mountains and how to survive on their hostile peaks and in their dark valleys.

And finally, the last desperate fight to save Berlin—the chaos as the command structure began to break down and weapons jammed or ran out of ammunition, and fights broke out over scraps of food or cigarettes. It had been, as he tried to break up one of these fights that, a stray bullet had strafed his head and shoulder knocking him senseless.

He had no recollection of how long he had lain there or of how he had ended up at the Königen Elisabeth Hospital.

Hanna made a thick soup of lentils and the last of the sausages, promising herself that she would join the bread queue early next morning on her way back from work. She didn't know that it would be her last shift at the Königen Elisabeth.

Königen Elisabeth Hospital: April 1945

That night, the Russians arrived swarming through the empty corridors and wards looking for things to steal as they went. Hanna locked the door to the ward where the last of their patients had been gathered and stood behind it listening to the sound of heavy boots and rough male voices approaching along the corridor.

Her colleague, Giesela, was doing her best to reassure two patients who, though very badly wounded, were conscious and aware of what was happening. It didn't take long for the soldiers to break down the door and storm the ward. One held the nurses at gunpoint while others dragged the helpless patients outside.

When the last of the patients had been removed, two of the soldiers returned and grabbed Hanna and Giesela, pinning their arms behind their backs. A rancid smell of stale sweat and alcohol invaded Hanna's nostrils, making her want to retch. Her legs had begun to tremble and she could feel a trickle of urine running down her thigh.

The soldier who had been holding the gun to their heads, began loosening his trousers signalling the start of a well-practiced assault. He ripped Giesela's skirt while his leering colleagues held the terrified women still. All of a sudden, Hanna became aware of a furious looking officer advancing across the ward.

The two soldiers holding the nurses saw him and immediately released their grip while the officer turned on the would-be rapist and pistol whipped him across the face and genitals leaving the man doubled up in agony on the floor.

"Allez…Vite, vite!" The officer shouted in halting French waving his pistol in the general direction of the door. "Allez, toute de suite!"

It took a moment or two before Hanna and Giesela realised that he was speaking to them and they ran as if their lives depended on it. As they left the hospital grounds, they heard a series of shots.

"Do you think the officer has just shot these awful soldiers?" Giesela gasped.

"No. There were too many shots for that," Hanna replied through tears.

"The patients…Oh no! Oh surely not!"

Hanna didn't reply, she just kept running.

Life in the Russian Sector

Just trying to stay alive in the months that followed the Russian invasion of Berlin was a desperate and terrifying struggle. Most of the buildings on the street where Hanna and Hans Dietrich lived had been reduced to ghostly skeletons. Jagged chimney stacks reached precariously towards the sky, grim sentinels guarding mountains of rubble, broken lives and broken belongings.

The windows facing the front of Hanna's block had been blown out and the apartments looted by drunken soldiers. Miraculously, her rear-facing apartment had been overlooked, but the miracle would not last for long. There was no running water or electricity and her days were spent in queues searching for food while trying to avoid the vodka-laced advances of the occupying troops.

She and Dietrich shared the only bed in her flat. They were not in love—humiliation and the daily battle for survival had robbed Berliners of the capacity for romance—but she and Dietrich did find brief solace in the warmth of each other's bodies.

Hanna finally found a job in a run-down clinic near the ruined Reichstag. Pay, if and when it arrived, was issued in debased currency or coupons for food which could not be found. Hans Dietrich struggled with enforced captivity and the long empty hours while Hanna worked. Debilitating panic attacks whenever he heard an unfamiliar noise only added to his sense of frustration.

His shoulder wound was not healing properly and he knew Hanna was right when she said that if he were stopped on the street, his age and injuries would mark him out as a former soldier. In the unlikely event that he escaped summary execution, he would be sent to a Soviet prisoner-of-war camp or press-ganged into one of the forced labour squads clearing bomb sites.

His chances of surviving either for more than a few days would have been slim. Hanna never knew whether she would return home to find him slumped in apathy or feverishly devising plans for escaping the Russian Sector and making for the family estate in Bavaria.

He became fractious if Hanna asked how he planned to navigate road blocks without documents permitting him to travel; how he would find out whose victorious army controlled which of the German regions he would need to pass through along the way; and how he might find or pay for transport.

Making the 600 kilometre journey on foot would have challenged a fit man and Hans Dietrich was half starved and sick. He would find answers to none of these questions sitting around in a flat, so he began to slip out while Hanna was at work in search of information. He called it scavenging and reassured Hanna that he avoided main roads, making his way cautiously through derelict buildings.

Some days he would return with a few pieces of wood for a stove they could not light in case the smoke revealed that people were living in the partially destroyed building, and once he came home with three eggs—an undreamed of luxury—which they had to whisk and drink raw for the same reason.

What alarmed Hanna most, was that he was meeting with a group of former soldiers, all intent on escape from the Russian Sector. He reassured her that they were being careful, never meeting in the same place twice. One person stood on guard and they always arrived and left separately. Hanna had not been reassured, but could do nothing to stop it.

By early autumn, Hanna knew she was pregnant and the worry of how she was going to be able to look after a child as well as Hans Dietrich almost pushed her to breaking point. She would have to tell him, it was his right to know, yet she sensed it would only add to his sense of guilt and worthlessness.

Returning from a fruitless search for bread one day, she steeled herself to tell him, and to reassure him that somehow they would all manage. Instead, she found his broken, lifeless body, at the entrance to their building. A passing Russian patrol had heard voices coming from the basement of a derelict factory and had lain in wait for the group to disperse.

Hans Dietrich had been followed and tossed down the stairwell as he unlocked the door of Hanna's flat. She stayed with his body, his head on her lap, past caring what happened to her, past caring about anything. She had no idea how long she sat on the cold pavement—was it hours or days—until a Russian truck arrived and German prisoners dragged his body from her arms to take it away for mass burial.

The driver would not tell her where they were taking him, and despite her efforts over the years, she never found his last resting place.

She supposed she should feel lucky given the appalling alternative. The Russian sergeant whose men had broken into her apartment turned up just after Hans Dietrich had been taken away. He looked around and decided to take sole ownership of the apartment and of the woman who lived there, sending his grumbling men packing.

This meant that Hanna was subject to the unwanted sexual advances of one man, rather than being gang raped on a regular basis as so many German women were in those dark days. Grim as the next few months were, Grigori provided some sort of precarious protection and he often brought food home. One day in January 1946, he went out and never returned.

She didn't look for him. Magdalena was born in April and Hanna thanked a God she no longer believed in that Magdalena was Hans Dietrich's daughter, not the child of war.

Chapter 7
London, October 1994

The Foreign and Commonwealth Office in King Charles Street had never seemed so vast and forbidding as it did on this cloudy, autumn morning, as if the very structure itself were turning its back on her. Ushered along a featureless corridor to a hard chair and instructed to wait, Angharad struggled to dominate waves of debilitating panic.

This was the day she had been dreading; the day when she would learn the outcome of the official investigation into her relationship with Amir Rashid. Standing silently beside her was the lawyer provided by The First Division Association—her Union.

After what felt like an eternity, a door opened at the far end of the corridor and a tall woman with grey hair and heavy, rimmed glasses walked towards her and introduced herself as an Assistant Secretary, appointed since Angharad's suspension from duty four months previously.

"I am sorry to have kept you waiting, Miss Wilson, but we are ready for you now."

Angharad did not recognise either of the men sitting at the polished mahogany table in the room where her fate would be pronounced. Introductions were made and the Assistant

Secretary said that she would chair the meeting. The two representatives from human resources were there as observers.

For some bizarre reason, Anya suddenly recalled a scene from a TV crime series in which a police chief under investigation stated that he would only take questions from officers of his own rank or above. Clearly, the FCO had gone for the minimum option in her case.

Time would tell whether this low key assembly meant that her fate was to be a severe reprimand followed by eternal banishment to the Stationary Office, immediate dismissal, or a charge of treason.

Allowing the heavy glasses to slip to the bridge of her nose, the chairwoman began to read from an official document, "Following extensive investigation, we accept Miss Wilson's assertion that she was unaware of Dr Amir Rashid's true identity when she embarked on a relationship with him in November 1993 and remained so throughout that relationship. We accept that there has been no further contact between Miss Wilson and Dr Rashid since his exposure and immediate recall to Teheran in June of this year."

"However, there are many instances in which Miss Wilson's conduct in the period November 1993 to June 1994 fell well below that expected of an experienced diplomat and could potentially have placed the security of the United Kingdom at risk.

- Knowing that Dr Rashid was a national of a foreign state which does not have diplomatic links with the United Kingdom, Miss Wilson failed to carry out due diligence to determine whether his cover story was a true representation of his circumstances. She simply accepted his account of his status as a Persian emigré who had elected to stay on in Rome after graduating from medical school.

- As an experienced diplomat, Miss Wilson would have been well aware of the risks of entrapment, yet at no point did she query why a successful, 45-year-old hospital consultant would seek to enter into a relationship with her."

"Objection!" Angharad's lawyer had suddenly burst into life. "I insist that this charge is deleted. It is irrelevant, unsubstantiated, and offensive." The terse litany continued unabated without reference to the lawyer's outburst.

- "Miss Wilson did not query or investigate Dr Rashid's many unexplained absences in the period January to March 1994, even on an occasion when she discovered that he had lied to her about his whereabouts. She accepted his excuse that he had been ending a previous relationship because he was in love with her, when in reality, he was in Cairo meeting his Iranian contact.
- Miss Wilson brought Dr Rashid onto embassy property on 19 January and to the Ambassador's Residence on 28 May 1994. On both occasions, Dr Rashid was found wandering unaccompanied around embassy property, contravening security regulations. The Embassy security Officer warned Miss Wilson that he did not trust Dr Rashid and instructed her to break off relations with him.

Miss Wilson chose to ignore this advice."

"Objection! When the security officer told my client that he did not trust Dr Rashid, my client asked what evidence he had for his suspicions, and was told he had none, just 'instinct borne of experience'. On the second occasion, she was told not to bring Dr Rashid back onto embassy property, but she was only advised, not instructed to break off relations with him."

"I insist that this charge is amended because at no time did the security officer provide any evidence to back his suspicions. Had he done so, we would not be here today." Once again, there was no response to the lawyer's intervention."

- "In the period April to June 1994, in contravention of FCO rules, Miss Wilson allowed Dr Rashid to reside at her embassy apartment in Rome without seeking appropriate clearance.
- On at least one occasion in the period April to June 1994, Miss Wilson gave Dr Rashid unsupervised access to her official laptop computer."

At this point, the chairwoman raised her head and looked directly at Angharad.

"We very much regret that the severity of these charges, irrespective of objections raised by your Counsel, leave us no option but to terminate your employment with the Foreign and Commonwealth Office." Angharad felt the room swirl around her, barely hearing the concluding remarks.

"You will receive written confirmation of this decision and the reasons for it. However, in recognition of your earlier exemplary service, our acceptance that you were unaware of Dr Rashid's identity, and that no classified information appears to have been exchanged, no formal charges will be brought against you. It has been agreed that you may retain your Civil Service pension rights. Is there anything you want to say?"

Angharad fled from the room and down the corridor ignoring calls telling her that she should be accompanied out of the building. Her lawyer caught up with her outside and led her round the corner to a bench in St James's Park, returning a few moments later with two cups of coffee.

"Do you want to appeal?"

"On what grounds? The charges are substantially true and they have decided that ignorance of Amir's identity does not excuse subsequent negligence and contraventions of regulations."

"We could appeal on the grounds that dismissal is too harsh given your preceding thirty years of 'exemplary service', to use their own words."

"Thank you, but I fear that wouldn't work. There are powerful voices behind the unfortunate woman who had to fire the shots today, not least my former ambassador's. There is nothing worse than having a security breach on your watch...unless it is a security breach uncovered by the CIA rather than by our own security services."

"I fear I have destroyed the ambassador's chances of a much sought-after knighthood and Everett Sympson would rather I were tried for treason and hanged than given a second chance. The person I am really sorry for is the security officer at the embassy. His career is shipwrecked because of my stupidity. Let's just leave things as they are, and thank you for your efforts on my behalf."

The walk to Green Park station seemed surreal, delayed shock and tears, alternating with amazement at the normality of things—workers heading reluctantly back to the office, toddlers grieving over skinned knees, lovers kissing, families of tourists laughing, children chasing pigeons. All oblivious to the titanic shift in the life of a slender woman slipping past them, head down, through London's Royal Parks.

At Green Park station, two newspaper headlines caught her eye—*The Times* headline, 'Edinburgh Academic Found Dead' in restrained contrast to *The Sun's*, 'Brutal Murder of Top Prof—Gay Hate Crime Suspected'. What prompted her to buy *The Times*? She was not normally drawn to reports of violent crime but there was something about this story…was it just the solace in knowing that worse things could happen than betrayal, financial ruin and professional disgrace?

Or was it a premonition that this case would one day turn her life around in ways she could not begin to imagine?

Chapter 8
Leigh-on-Sea,
Essex September 1995

Catherine Mitchell reluctantly closed the door on her childhood home on a sunny September morning in 1995. For a few moments, she stared unseeing at the faded blue paint as memories flooded back of the years when this house had represented safety—a place where she had been loved and where her lively intelligence had been encouraged and developed by her amazing aunt.

She could almost hear the laughter as she and her friends played in the garden or headed off into the copse behind the house—they had called it a forest then—to parody the adventures of 'The Famous Five'. It had been a tough few days clearing out the last of her aunt's belongings and that morning a local charity had arrived to take away the final items, including her childhood bed and a table.

On impulse, she had thrown a small chintz chair—her chair—into the back of her Audi hatchback instead of giving it away. She would put it in her dressing room in Edinburgh; then allowed herself a mischievous smile at the thought of placing it in the midst of the otherwise relentless good taste of her drawing room.

The furnishings in the house she shared with her husband, James, and two teenage children had largely been selected by her mother-in-law who feared, quite correctly, that Catherine's modest upbringing would have ill-prepared her for the task of furnishing a twelve-room mansion in Edinburgh's exclusive Grange district.

Beneath the dining room window, a single pink hollyhock stood sentinel, defying the gradual decline of a once beautiful garden, while its defeated colleagues lay sprawled over the unkempt grass. By the gate a huge, ornamental poppy had gone to seed, blissfully unaware of its precarious future should a new owner dislike its prolific abandon.

Catherine closed the gate without looking back and threw a plastic bag of odds and ends for the charity shop into the boot of the car alongside the little chair. The bag contained an almost new Loden coat, and as Catherine started the car, she felt again a pang of regret for having been so impatient with her aunt on the day they had bought that coat.

Catherine had not appreciated the rapid toll dementia had taken on her aunt's once acute mind, from simple forgetfulness in August to arriving in Edinburgh in late December with a suitcase full of summer clothes and no coat, 'because these were the clothes she had packed the last time she had come north'.

Her aunt was too small to fit one of Catherine's coats and she had flatly refused to go to Marks & Spencer or John Lewis to buy a coat on the grounds that new coats were too expensive and she 'wouldn't get the wear out of it'. The reluctant compromise had been the Oxfam shop in

Morningside. That was where they found the Loden coat which fitted perfectly.

However, Aunt Agnes declared the price tag of £50 excessive and Catherine had been rather sharp with her, over-ruling her protests and insisting she buy it. The atmosphere had been frosty as Catherine made a spur-of-the-moment donation for victims of drought in Ethiopia and signed the gift-aid form. She had dismissed her aunt's subsequent complaints about the coat hurting her legs as nothing more than petulance.

Catherine had been devastated by her aunt's death the following April—in many ways, she was still devastated and strangely rudderless in spite of having a loving family of her own.

Before setting out on the long journey home, she had to hand the house keys over to the estate agent in Southend-on-Sea, and the bag of odds and ends to the Oxfam shop. Half way towards Southend, she knew she wasn't ready to hand over the keys and turned her car towards the waterfront at Westcliff.

She parked the car and walked back along the shore to the Peterboat Inn at Leigh-on-Sea where she sat at an outside table and ordered a crab salad and a large glass of chilled white wine. How many evenings had she spent there with student friends, chatting and laughing while trying to make half a pint of beer last for hours?

She had wanted to keep the house, but James had said it was impractical. The children had always been happy to come to the Essex Coast while Aunt Agnes was alive, but at fourteen and sixteen, they had outgrown the attractions around Southend Pier and their former enthusiasm for Fish and Chips at Henry Higgins had been replaced by a preference for more sophisticated fare.

James had suggested selling the house and buying a property in France which the whole family could enjoy and where Catherine could spend the summer doing her research. He was kind and fully understood her grief for her aunt but he could never know how much that house had meant to her. He had been brought up in a secure home with parents and grandparents who adored him.

He had gone to a private school, holidayed abroad and already owned a flat and a car while he was at Durham University where they had met. Catherine's early childhood could not have been more different.

Her mind drifted to her early years and to the fading memory of her mother. Marianne Mitchell had been the apple of her father's eye. Highly intelligent and beautiful, she had won a scholarship to study languages at Edinburgh University.

She and her family had been in no doubt that a stellar career lay before her as an interpreter on a high-flying international stage. She far outshone her older sister, Agnes, who had returned from Durham with a broken heart—her boyfriend having died of cancer at the end of their second year—and a respectable 2.1 in History.

Agnes was destined to teach at the local High School for Girls while Marianne was destined to have the world at her feet. Or so everyone had thought.

During *Freshers' Week* for new students at Edinburgh University, Marianne was immediately drawn to the lifestyle of a fast crowd—young men and women with large trust funds behind them and already experienced in dodging the many pitfalls of life in the fast lane. Marianne had no such experience and by the end of her first year, cocaine, sex and alcohol had taken their toll on her work and she failed her exams.

Her shocked parents brought her back to Leigh-on-Sea for the summer but by the time she returned to university for the autumn re-sits, there was no denying that she was pregnant. There was a doctor in Edinburgh who performed illegal abortions, but he charged £100 and her pleas to her former friends fell on deaf ears. Men who had been bowled over by her beauty a year before had no wish to face paternity suits.

The women agreed 'she had never really been one of us!'. Marianne had no option but to tell her parents and she moved back home at the end of term.

Catherine was born the following March and spent the first eighteen months of her life with her grandparents. Lifestyle tensions within the household finally reached breaking point and Marianne announced she was going back to Edinburgh and taking Catherine with her. When no amount of pleading could convince Marianne to stay, or at least to leave Catherine behind, her distraught parents bought her a flat in Edinburgh.

Catherine's troubled memories of the next four years were confused. Happy times when her grandparents visited and times when she felt very alone and afraid when her mother was not around. Everything fell apart when she was six. Her mother had lost her job as a receptionist at the Bruntsfield Hotel and her grandfather's appeal to the hotel manager to give his daughter a second chance had fallen on deaf ears.

There had already been several 'second chances' and periodic irregularities in the takings had continued unabated.

That year, her grandparents had stayed on after Christmas, ostensibly so that her grandfather could finish decorating her bedroom and fitting new furniture.

The real reason had been to enable her grandparents to accompany her to school at the start of term and to talk to the head teacher about their concerns, leaving a sum of money in trust to cover the cost of her lunches and up-coming school trips. By then, they had become all too aware that money left with Marianne would not be spent on her child.

In spite of severe weather warnings, her grandparents had set off for home soon afterwards because her grandmother had a long-awaited hospital appointment. They had hoped to outrun the forecast snow but just south of the Scottish border, they were caught in a blizzard and died in a multiple collision when a lorry heading northwards skidded, ploughing into the line of cars crawling southwards.

By early spring, the flat had to be sold because Marianne 'had debts' and they moved into a grim two room apartment in Causewayside. Her mother worked nights at a bar somewhere near the port at Leith; there was little food in the house and frequently no coins for the electricity meter.

Catherine had lived for school holidays which she spent with her aunt, returning well fed and healthy with new clothes, reassuring the social worker alerted by concerned staff at her school that all was well. But all was not well and the worst times were the weeks when her school holidays did not coincide with her aunt's.

Her mother had lost her bar job and was working the streets, sometimes bringing men home late at night. It all came to a head during an exceptionally cold mid-term break in October. She hadn't seen her mother for days and was running out of survival tactics. She had gone to the Royal Commonwealth Pool every morning because children could swim free during the holidays and she could have a hot shower afterwards.

On two occasions, a friend's mother had taken her to the café after swimming, but she had asked too many questions about where Catherine's mother was, so she had avoided the woman after that. She spent most afternoons in the National Museum of Scotland where it was warm, returning home through fallen leaves on the Meadows as light was fading.

Sometimes the lady in the refreshment stall beside the play park would give her a left-over sandwich, but she too had started asking questions. One evening, hungry, cold and drenched by driving rain, Catherine couldn't take any more and went to her friend, Lucy's house.

Lucy's father had already made it clear that he did not want Catherine hanging around because 'she came from a bad home', but Lucy's mother took one look at the girl standing dripping on the doorstep and invited her in, gave her dry clothes and insisted that she stay for supper. Lucy and she overheard the heated conversation when her father returned.

"I'm sorry for the girl, but she can't stay here. We put ourselves at risk every time we send her home to what we know is an empty house. She is only eight after all. We should phone her social worker, it's their responsibility." Lucy's mother promised to do so next day, meantime her husband would need to give Catherine a lift home as they could not send her away on her own when it was dark and wet outside.

"This is exactly what I mean," Lucy's father had responded in exasperation. "I am a lawyer and you are asking me to drop an eight year old off at a flat we know will be empty. If anything were to happen to her, we could be in real trouble. This has to stop; she must not come here again."

"What's more, I don't want Lucy getting involved with the sort of people who hang around with Catherine's mother on the rare occasions when she is actually at home!"

With that, he ushered Catherine into his car and drove wordlessly to Causewayside. Catherine would never forget the overwhelming sense of shame and anger she had felt on that short journey. She couldn't wait to get out of the car, to escape the awful sense of being unwanted and worthless.

However, to her surprise and dismay, Lucy's father decided to accompany her to the flat. As they walked across the road, a thick-set man came hurtling out of the main entrance and ran off in the direction of the Meadows. Lucy's father became suspicious as he registered that the man wore nothing more than jeans and a tee shirt on that very cold and wet night.

He climbed the dark, musty stairway ahead of Catherine and, as he reached the second-floor landing, he saw that the door to the flat was open but there were no lights on inside.

"The meter will have run out of money," Catherine said, deeply embarrassed.

Lucy's father put some coins in the meter by the door and lights went on in the living room.

"Wait here," he said, moving cautiously into the room. Marianne lay sprawled across a rug beside the fireplace. She was naked from the waist down and a syringe lay on the floor beside her. Cigarette ends littered the battered coffee table and an empty bottle of vodka rolled around on the floor. A man's jacket was tossed in a corner.

"Stay there," he shouted as he heard the child move towards the door. "Your mother's not well, we need to go down to the car and call an ambulance." Catherine had wanted to go to her mother, but Lucy's father took her by the arm and set off down the stairs pulling her behind him.

He called the police and an ambulance from a sat phone in the car, then phoned his wife and asked her to send a taxi to take Catherine back to their house while he waited for the emergency services.

Aunt Agnes arrived the next day and took Catherine to a small hotel in town. She explained as gently as she could that Marianne had died because a bad person had given her some medicine that was too strong for her. Shock set in and Catherine had only the vaguest memories of visits by police and social workers, or of the Children's Hearing where it was decided that she should live with Aunt Agnes in Leigh-on-Sea.

All she could recall was a strange sense of elation as the London train set off from Waverley Station, and for years afterwards, she felt guilty because she was so happy; it seemed awful to be relieved that her mother was dead.

Now, sitting on the sea wall at the Peterboat Inn, she suddenly felt a rush of compassion for the wasted promise of her mother's life. She thought about how young her aunt had been when she gave up her freedom to look after a small girl.

She remembered with gratitude how good growing up in Leigh-on-Sea had been, the friends she had made at school and at the Youth Club at St Mary's Church—the sight of its ancient bell tower rising above the cliff top a strangely comforting reminder of the view from her old bedroom window. She remembered helping her aunt to arrange the flowers for Easter Sunday and helping her serve teas after morning service.

She remembered trips in her aunt's ancient Morris Minor to visit historical sites all over England and the north of France. She remembered help with her homework and bedtime cocoa sitting in her special chair—the chair which now lay in the boot of her car. How could her husband and children ever understand what that house had meant to her?

Brought back to the present by a crowd of laughing youngsters, she looked at her watch and saw with astonishment that it was five pm. The estate agent and charity shop would be closed by the time she had walked back to her car and driven the short distance to Southend. It wasn't a problem.

She would push the keys through the estate agent's letter box and leave the bag of clothes outside the charity shop. If some impoverished person decided to steal the contents overnight, she hoped they would find them useful.

It would have astonished her to know that her aunt's coat would become a key piece of evidence in a murder investigation. Her aunt would have found it absolutely thrilling.

Chapter 9
Bavaria, 1990

"His Excellency wants to see you. You must come at once, he is dying." The butler's cold, clipped tones betrayed no emotion, no compassion but that was the way things had always been in his father's house. Reluctantly, Monsignor Hans Albrecht von Seidel made his way to the university car park and climbed into his Passat.

What to say at the end to a father he had always feared and disliked, to the father who had made no secret of the fact he despised his youngest son and his decision to join the church instead of assuming his responsibilities to the family estate and business?

As his car pulled up in front of the faux baroque frontage of Schloss Stauffensee, he felt a familiar revulsion at his father's grandiose remodelling of the original Palladian Villa Stauffensee, enlarged to correspond to his father's rising status in the Nazi party and the favours conferred on him by Adolf Hitler in the 1930s.

He found his father lying on a day bed in his study, his sister, Stefania, at his side. Faint shafts of sunshine filtered through drawn curtains casting small pools of light onto the rich Turkish carpet; a dimmed lamp by the bedside was the only other source of light. His father's once imposing physique was reduced to little more than skin and bones and a tremor played on his hands.

The heavy gold ring he always wore lay loosely around an emaciated finger. His cheeks were sunken but the predatory stare of his cold, hard eyes still had the ability to create fear. "Leave us, Stefania, I need to talk to Albrecht alone." Stefania rose casting a fleeting, concerned glance at Albrecht as she left the room.

"I am sorry if I have called you away from your academic pursuits." The veiled sarcasm was not lost on his son. "I wouldn't have troubled you at all, but you are my only surviving son and, regrettably, the one least fitted to carry out my wishes."

"However, as there is no one else, you will just have to make the best of it—it's not a job that can be left to your sister with her mind full of philanthropic nonsense no doubt inspired by you."

As his father spoke, Albrecht listened in mounting horror. Despite the cloying heat in the room, he felt cold. He wanted to silence the dry, rasping voice. He didn't want to hear, he didn't want to know and he didn't want to do what was asked of him.

Finally, his father slipped the ring off his finger, fumbling as he attempted to put it in his son's hand. Albrecht stared in utter revulsion at the sinister object lying in his palm. It seemed to overwhelm his very being, glinting menacingly as its previous owner had so often done. For a long time, he sat in silence, a silence broken only by his father's increasingly laboured breathing.

Finally, remembering his vocation, he asked if his father wished to receive the last rites. "I have no need of your incantations," were the last words his father ever spoke.

Albrecht moved his chair across to the window and looked again at the heavy, ugly ring. How often had he felt that rip across his cheek when yet again he had failed to live up to his father's expectations? He was, after all, 'the replacement child'; born to replace Hans Jurgen, his father's favourite who had died of pneumonia, aged eight.

But Albrecht's father had hated him from the day he was born, blaming him for the death of his mother in childbirth, blaming him for being a frail, gentle child, blaming him for failing to live up to the ghostly paragon, Jurgen. Until the age of nine, he was also routinely compared unfavourably with two much older war hero brothers.

One of whom, Hans Dietrich, had won the Iron Cross fighting with Rommel in Africa and had apparently died a hero's death as the Russians stormed Berlin. The other, Hans Peter, ceased to be a fallen hero in 1946 following a raft of unwelcome revelations about his wartime activities. He was never spoken of again and was presumed to be dead.

The last time Albrecht saw his brothers was in 1942. He was afraid of Peter who took a sadistic delight in tormenting him, frequently reminding him that he had killed their mother. Albrecht recalled Dietrich standing up for him one day, shouting, "Leave the child alone, it's not his fault that mother died. If you want to blame someone, blame father."

As Stefania tucked him up in bed that night, he was still trying to make sense of this latest revelation. "Dietrich says it was father not me who killed Mummy. Is that true?" Stefania sat down on the bed and explained that it was no one's fault that Mummy had died.

Daddy and Mummy had both wanted another child, but childbirth was difficult and Mummy had a weak heart. He remembered thinking how hard it was to know what to believe. And it was even harder now to look at this ring and the awful legacy his father had bequeathed him.

He was jolted from his feverish thoughts by a sudden rattle as his father fought and failed to catch breath. Albrecht moved quietly over and closed his father's unseeing eyes, murmuring a prayer to an ever-merciful God that he might find something redeemable in Hans Ludvig's departed soul.

That night, Stefania had begged him to throw the ring away, to drop it into the lake, to forget the whole thing. She had begged him not to find the vault to which it was the key.

"Everything in that vault has been missing now for almost fifty years. The people who owned whatever is there are probably dead, it's just too dangerous. Who knows what you might find. Father had no right asking you to clear up his mess. He was a monster who ruined your childhood and now he is going to ruin your life. Please, Albrecht…"

With a heavy heart, he reminded her that the vault probably contained works of art that were part of the patrimony of all humanity, and other works which rightly belonged to the survivors or heirs of the countless people deported to the camps. The vault had to be opened and its contents returned to their rightful owners.

"But what will happen to us? Remember what it was like when the MFAA* descended on us at the end of the war and the Monuments Men turned our house over and dug up the grounds looking for paintings they believed Peter had removed from trainloads of stolen art destined for Göring or Hitler."

"You were too young to be interrogated, but father and I were questioned for days on end. It was terrifying, and Hanna, Magdalena and the children could be caught up in this too this time. Please, Albrecht, nothing good can come of this."

"Stefania, this is too big for us to bury. That vault has to be opened."

"Then let the Turkish police do it, or Interpol or whoever. Just send them the ring and the address."

"I promise you, I will take the ring to the appropriate authorities as soon as possible, but first, I need to visit the vault so that we know exactly what it contains."

"But suppose Hans Peter is still alive. He will know about the vault; he was probably in this with father before the war. The ring was safe while it was in Germany as it would have been too risky for Peter to return here even under a false identity, but you travel all over the world. He could track you down when you are in Scotland with Charles, or in Turkey or Syria…"

"Stefania, Peter isn't alive. At the end of the war, everyone was looking for him. The British because of his role in the massacre of British prisoners of war at Le Paradis, The War Crimes Tribunal and *Simon Wiesenthal for his part in the deportation of Jews and the confiscation of Jewish property, the MFAA and Museum Directors across Europe for the theft of art works, the Italians for his part in the massacre of civilians in Sant'Anna di Stazzema."

"If he was alive, he would have been found unless he has been hiding with a lost tribe in the Amazon all these years. In any case, he would be in his 70s by now, and even I am no longer scared of him."

"Will you at least speak to Hanna and Charles before you do anything rash?"

"No, Stefania," he said kindly, "we can't drag anyone else into this mess."

The Allies set up the Monuments Fine Arts and Archives Program (MFAA) in 1944 to search for monuments, fine art, antiquities and archives stolen by the Nazis, especially those stolen by the ERR—the Einsatzstab Reichsleiter Rosenberg Institute for the Occupied Territories. The expert investigators were known as The Monuments Men.

Simon Wiesenthal was a Jewish Holocaust survivor, writer and founder of the Jewish Historical Documentation Centre in Austria. He dedicated his life to tracking down Nazi war criminals.

She was crying softly as he left making him hate his father even more. He hated upsetting Stefania who, he knew, had given up her own young life to be a mother to him. She had stayed at home to look after him rather than go to university. She had protected him and loved him.

There had been a young man, but he had disappeared for ever on the long retreat through a merciless Russian winter. There had never been anyone else. Once Albrecht had left home for university, she threw herself into work with a local orphanage—the philanthropic activity her father so despised. In a terrified corner of her mind, instinct told her that Hans Peter was still alive.

Chapter 10
Edinburgh, 1990

Everyone who knew him agreed that Charles Gibson was a delightful man who wore his erudition lightly. In the jealous, ambitious academic world, he was an anomaly. In spite of his vast learning and international reputation in the field of Ottoman Art and History, he had never sought promotion and was always ready to support colleagues and students as they embarked on their own research or careers.

He lived in the house where he had been born, until recently sharing it with his mother, a redoubtable classicist who had fought tooth and nail, until dementia intervened, to preserve the place of Latin and Greek in the Scottish school curriculum. He was a sociable man and his dinner parties were a legend among his friends.

As far as family and friends knew, he had never been romantically involved with anyone, male or female, but he was very close to Monsignor Hans Albrecht von Seidel and his family. For many years, Charles and his mother had spent Christmas and Easter in Bavaria with the von Seidel family and Albrecht, often accompanied by his sister and niece, Magdalena, came to Scotland every summer to attend the Edinburgh Festival.

Christmas 1990 would be the first time in three years that Charles had been able to go to Bavaria as he had cared for his mother until her death a few months earlier following a long and distressing illness. To his delight, he had just learned that Hanna, Magdalena and her family would also be there. What an amazing story that had been.

In 1989, just after the Berlin Wall had come down, the von Seidel family had received an astonishing letter from a woman called Hanna Brandt.

Dear Baron von Seidel, Stefania and Hans Albrecht,

I don't know if you will remember me. In the summer of 1939, I spent two weeks at your home with Hans Dietrich and other friends from Heidelberg University. We didn't know then how soon war would tear our carefree lives apart. I lost touch with Dietrich after he joined the army and soon I, too, left university to join the nursing corps—I had been studying medicine.

In late February 1945, I was working at the Königen Elizabeth Hospital in Berlin when Dietrich was admitted with serious wounds. In April, the Russians shelled the hospital and as Dietrich had still not recovered sufficiently to be discharged, I took him to my apartment near the Alexander Platz to recuperate. These were terrifying times in Berlin.

One day in late April, Hans Peter appeared urging Dietrich to leave Berlin with him but Dietrich refused to go. On 20 July, I returned home to find Dietrich's body on the pavement outside my apartment. He had been killed by Russian soldiers. I hid his Iron Cross and Identity Tag under the floorboards and would like to return these to you now that it is possible to make contact with the West once more.

Dietrich and I weren't married, and he was too ill to think about falling in love, but we have a lovely daughter, Magdalena, who was born in March 1946. We aren't looking for anything from the family. Magdalena is a successful lawyer in Leipzig, married with two children. I am retired now, but still living in my apartment in Berlin.

Please let me know what you would like me to do with Dietrich's Iron Cross and Identity Tag.

Yours sincerely,
Hanna Brandt

Hans Ludvig's reaction was predictable. "She's obviously looking for money. Find out how much she wants for the Iron Cross and Identity Tag and get them. As for the daughter, she is more likely to be a Russian soldier's brat than Hans Dietrich's. We don't want anything to do with her or her mother."

Albrecht and Stefania ignored this command and drove straight to Berlin.

Chapter 11
Hotel Sospiri,
Sultanhamet, Istanbul
November 1991

Ayşe Demirel had just finished her early morning shift at the Hotel Sospiri when two burly African men in dark jackets and sunglasses pushed in through the main entrance. Behind Ayşe, her colleague, Kemal, stood ready to take over but, more importantly, he had decided that this was the day when he would finally find the courage to ask her out.

What had tormented his thoughts over many weeks was the possibility that she might refuse if he didn't get it just right. To invite her for coffee might seem rather tame, to invite her to the cinema or to dinner might seem too much too soon. However, a perfect solution had just presented itself— a fireworks display which could be viewed perfectly from Taksim Square with the prospect of relaxing later in one of the fashionable cafés nearby.

Lost in thought, he didn't notice the two men at the counter asking Ayşe none too politely where they would find Charles Gibson.

"I'm sorry, Dr Gibson has already checked out," she answered brightly. Kemal, checking the bookings on screen, was about to contradict her when he felt a sharp kick on his ankle. He remained silent.

"Where did he go?" The larger of the two men demanded.

"Izmir…I am sure he was going to Izmir. He asked for directions and I told him to go to Hyderapasha where he could catch a train or a ferry to Izmir."

Kemal looked at Ayşe in astonishment. Giving out information—even wrong information—about guests was against all the hotel rules. Furthermore, Dr Gibson probably knew how to get to Izmir better than most Istanbülüs.

"Give me Gibson's address!" The man said, his fist coming down hard on the polished desk.

"I am sorry, we cannot…" Kemal began.

"Give me the fucking address if you want this bitch to walk out of here in one piece!"

As the man vaulted the desk, Kamal shut down the computer but before he could do anything more, the man had Ayşe in a tight neck lock.

"The fucking address or she's history!" His companion said in a low, menacing voice.

As Kemal's fingers fumbled to restart the computer, he heard the faint sound of police sirens in the distance. The hotel security officer, witnessing the scene unfold on video, had pressed the panic button. The assailants heard the sirens too and made for the door, disappearing into the narrow lanes behind the hotel.

Finally emerging from the safety of the back office in time to greet the police, the hotel manager told his two badly shaken colleagues to go into the lounge for coffee while they waited to be questioned. "What was all that about Izmir?" Kemal asked.

"I knew at once these men were not the sort of people Dr Gibson associated with, so I told them he had already checked out. I said he'd gone to Izmir, because it takes ages to get from here to Hyderapasha through the morning traffic, plus they wouldn't have known whether Dr Gibson had taken a train or a ferry and it's a long journey either way."

"And now they are left with the problem of how to find one man in a city the size of Izmir, especially as he isn't there!"

"You could just have said we can't give out information about our hotel guests."

"Well, you saw how successful quoting hotel policy was when you tried."

"But what made you suspect they were up to no good right from the start?"

"It was because…but, of course, you don't know, it was your day off yesterday. It was because Dr Gibson's friend, the lovely German professor, was found dead in his hotel room yesterday morning. The police say it was murder and poor Dr Gibson was in a terrible state last night. He'd had to speak to the police and identify the body."

"Then he had to phone his friend's family to tell them what had happened. Poor man! I am sure the two African guys are connected with the murder in some way."

They had just started to recount their story to a young police officer when an older man in civilian clothes entered, introducing himself as Inspector Djavid from the serious crimes unit. He made the young policeman nervous. Inspector

Djavid asked him to continue his questioning, interrupting frequently for clarification.

'What language did they speak? Was their English fluent? Did they give any indication of why they wanted to see Dr Gibson? What made you suspicious of them? Could you describe the men fully—age, height, build, colour, ethnicity? What were they wearing? Was anyone else with them or waiting for them outside? Did they have a car? Did Monsignor von Seidel call on Dr Gibson at any time during his stay?'

By the time the interview ended and Inspector Djavid had gone off to study the video footage, both receptionists and the young police officer felt as if they had just tried to defend a poorly argued PhD thesis! It was already late afternoon as Ayşe and Kemal left the hotel. Somehow it didn't seem the right time to suggest going to a fireworks display.

Chief Inspector Kadir Demercol studied the hunched-up figure before him with a mixture of compassion and frustration. Perched on the edge of an uncomfortable hotel bedroom chair, Charles Gibson was struggling to control the trembling in his left leg and an overwhelming sense of panic and despair.

He wanted to cry, he needed to go to the bathroom, he wanted to flee—nothing, absolutely nothing in his quiet academic world had prepared him for the anguish of this moment.

"Can you please take us through the events of the last week again," the chief inspector asked as patiently as he could. "And if you can think of any reason why someone might want to kill your friend, now is the time to tell me."

Charles looked up, unbidden tears blurring his vision. "I don't think I can add anything to the statement I gave to Inspector Djavid yesterday."

"Dr Gibson, two men called here today looking for you. Most likely these were the men who killed Albrecht von Seidel. They called because they obviously believe that before he died, Monsignor von Seidel gave you information or an object that they want so badly they will torture and kill for it."

"They would have found you were it not for a quick-thinking receptionist who didn't like the look of the callers. And they would not have questioned you nicely! So, from the start please, beginning with what brought you both to Istanbul."

"Albrecht and I have been friends for over thirty years. He is, he was an authority on Byzantine religious art. My field is Ottoman Art and History. We were both invited to the expert seminar on the tomb chamber recently discovered by building contractors laying the foundations for a new mosque in Trebizond."

"I read about the find," said Demercol brusquely. "And where did this seminar take place?"

"It was held at the Istanbul Archaeology Museum in Sultanhamet and on site at Trebizond. The chamber was originally used as a Christian church by Venetian merchants after the Fall of Constantinople in 1453. Two centuries later, the frescoed walls were plastered over when the upper building was transformed into a mosque."

"The plaster has now been removed and Albrecht was there to study the frescoes. My interest was in relation to the more puzzling find—the shrouded but unburied remains of two young women wearing magnificent Ottoman jewellery."

Sensing that Charles was relaxing into professorial mode, Demercol steered the conversation back to the present.

"Did anything strike you as unusual in Monsignor von Seidel's recent behaviour?"

"Albrecht seemed to have a lot on his mind following his father's death in December last year. True, it was a huge estate to settle, but relatively simple in that the beneficiaries were his two surviving children, Albrecht and Stefania and his only granddaughter, Magdalena. I remember Albrecht saying to me, 'Even in death, my father torments me!'"

"All last week, he seemed distracted and, unusually for him, missed several seminar sessions. Normally, faced with a find of this importance, he would have given it his undivided attention. When we last spoke, he seemed stressed, almost frightened."

"We had planned to have dinner together yesterday evening, then an early start today to carry out some more research in Trebizond before returning to Munich and Edinburgh respectively at the end of the week. However, Albrecht called at my hotel late yesterday afternoon to say that he couldn't join me for dinner and that we would have to cancel the trip to Trebizond."

"He seemed agitated, apologised profusely and said he had to deal with a serious problem related to his father's estate. When I asked if I could help in any way, he thanked me and said that he didn't want to involve me; that his father had been an evil monster in life and remained so in death; and that he had no idea how best to resolve the moral dilemma he had been left to sort out."

"You knew his father. How would you describe him?"

"In Albrecht's own words. Hans Ludvig von Seidel was a most unpleasant man. A Nazi sympathiser and friend of Herman Göring, he dealt in fine art becoming enormously wealthy during the 1930s. There were convincing rumours that he worked with Alfred Rosenberg and Göring on the seizure of Jewish art collections."

"After the war, he was investigated by MFAA as they attempted to trace stolen works of art but nothing was ever proved. He was clever at covering his tracks. Albrecht was a very different kind of man and his decision to become a priest was his way of distancing himself from his father and all he stood for."

"What was the moral dilemma that Albrecht's father had left him to sort out?"

"He wouldn't tell me."

"Do you think Hans Ludvig may have told Albrecht about the location of stolen art just before he died?"

"He might have done; it would certainly explain the change in Albrecht's behaviour, but he refused to say what was troubling him."

"Did Monsignor von Seidel give you anything to keep for him—a key, a code, an address or anything else that his assailants might be looking for?"

Charles felt the faint pressure of Albrecht's ring in his inside pocket. "No," he said, honouring Albrecht's last request, yet far from sure that concealment was the right thing to do.

Chapter 12
Izmir, Turkey, 1991

Driving down a country road near Kemalpasha, Orhan Erdogan was quietly cursing his mother. It was ten-thirty at night, a time when all sensible farmers should be in bed, yet here he was making a 60 kilometre round trip in response to his mother's latest panic phone call—this time about intruders in her courtyard.

Although, these calls always proved to be false alarms, he could not risk ignoring tearful pleas from the eighty-nine year old widow. As he turned a sharp corner, his headlights picked out an overturned car on the side of the road. He decided to stop and taking the powerful torch he kept in the glove compartment, he got out of his car to see if anyone needed help.

The overturned car was partially burnt out, wedged between a thick hedge and the embankment—*Young idiots joy riding*, he thought. An acrid smell hung in the air and the mangled metalwork was still warm. Cautiously, he shone the torch into the interior and immediately retched—to the considerable annoyance of the forensics team called to the scene an hour later.

The beam revealed two bodies, charred beyond recognition, limbs contorted into a grotesque arabesque. The nearest phone was at his mother's house and ten minutes later, he swept past the astonished woman left standing in the doorway while he called the police in Izmir. For a moment, she thought her son had taken her tale of intruders more seriously than he usually did.

Police Headquarters, Istanbul: November, 1991: Sunday

Chief Inspector Kadir Demercol rested a well-manicured hand on the receiver of the phone on his desk. He had just concluded the third depressing phone call of the morning. The first call had been from his superior demanding an update on the case, and reminding Demercol that an immediate arrest was imperative.

The death of a respected German aristocrat in an upmarket Istanbul hotel was bad for the reputation of the Turkish police, bad for the tourist industry and any delay in identifying and apprehending the culprit was not to be contemplated. The second call was from his superior informing him that Prime Minister Demirol needed an answer before his scheduled meeting with Chancellor Helmut Kohl in Berlin the following week.

The third call was from Inspector Djavid. Traffic police in Bursa had just found a car abandoned on the verge of the Bursa to Eskişehir road. The car was burnt out; it had been reported stolen from the Hyderapasha district of Istanbul earlier the previous day. Inside were the bodies of two men whose fatal injuries did not correspond to the damage to the vehicle. They carried no identification.

Demercol swore softly—in all probability his only leads in the murder investigation had just been silenced. Of course, these could be two quite different men, but that likelihood was remote, the coincidences were too great and they had been found barely one kilometre from the main Istanbul to Izmir highway.

He was suddenly overcome by the desire to walk out of the office and go home to join his wife and children for lunch. He could almost smell the roasting lamb and aromatic spices, see the dishes of aubergine and sweet tomato, the little pastries filled with goats cheese and herbs, the baklava dripping with honey and the tiny glasses of rich, aromatic coffee.

His mother and father would be there and he could imagine how the conversation was already developing. As sole heir to one of the wealthiest families in Istanbul; a family which could trace its lineage back over a thousand years and had produced three Grand Viziers and a military commander who had led his troops to the gates of Vienna, Kadir Demercol did not need to work—as his mother seldom missed an opportunity to point out.

Home was a historic wooden villa in Nişanştaşi, externally authentic, but internally modernised to the exacting standards of his beloved wife. His mother would be in full flow. "I don't know why he feels the need to work, but if that is what he wants, why the police? Why does he not join the board of any one of a hundred companies who would fall over themselves to have a Demercol as a Trustee."

And that was precisely why he had chosen a harder career path. He did not want to be a token 'Demercol', he wanted to show his worth where his name meant nothing—and it meant absolutely nothing to his commander who had come up the hard way and who was deeply suspicious of anyone who could trace their ancestry further back than *Atatürk.

Three days later, in his office in Istanbul, Chief Inspector Demercol read the report from his colleagues in Izmir with mounting frustration. The police had found no identification on or near the bodies. The car was stolen and the best the pathologist could come up with was that they were male, heavily built and of African origin.

They had been shot neatly through the back of the neck before the blaze. The gun, cartridges and bullets were nowhere to be found. No one had reported the men missing, and responses to an urgent request passed round embassies in Ankara and Consulates in Istanbul revealed nothing of consequence to the investigation.

Instinct told him that these were the men who had been seen in the lobby of the Hotel Ariel the night Hans Albrecht von Seidel was murdered and who had come looking for Dr Gibson at the Hotel Sospiri the next day, but with no clues as to their identity or the identity of whoever sent them, he was no further forward. This was not what his commander or the prime minister would want to hear.

Mustafa Kemal Ataturk was a soldier, revolutionary and statesman. He was the founding father of the independent Republic of Turkey following the fall of the Ottoman Empire in 1923

Izmir Harbour

A tall man with a badly scarred face stared out unseeingly over Izmir harbour, overwhelmed by desperation, shaking

115

after recent catastrophic events and angry, very angry at his two former associates. In the days when he had been a wealthy land owner in Argentina, he could afford highly professional security guards and enforcers—men with a past to hide and an intense loyalty to their employer.

Sadly, these days were long gone and now he was an almost penniless fugitive living in Mogadishu and reduced to employing street thugs to carry out his more questionable errands. He needed his father's ring, the ring with the seal and code. The seal and code he needed to gain access to his horde of stolen art concealed in a high security storage vault in the Beyoglu district of Istanbul.

By rights, the ring should have passed to him on his father's death, but as he had been declared missing presumed dead after the courts at Nuremberg had finally given up trying to trace him, the ring had passed to his youngest brother, Albrecht—two intervening brothers having died prematurely; Hans Jurgen aged eight in 1936 (a death he had precipitated and preferred not to dwell upon); and Hans Dietrich as Russian troops raged through bomb-ravaged Berlin in 1945.

He had destroyed the Mogadishans' few personal belongings and their false identity documents. At seventy-three years old, he had had to force them to stop the stolen car on an embankment bordering a quiet country road, shoot them, collect the cartridges and bullets, push the car into the ditch and set it alight. Then he had to walk five kilometres to Bornova and take a public service bus to Izmir.

He was too old for exertions of that sort. He felt no remorse, as he had felt no remorse for his part in the massacre of 94 British prisoners of war at Le Paradis in France in 1940, or of 560 Italian men, women and children at St Anna di

Stazzema in 1944. He simply felt anger. He had sent the Mogadishans to persuade his brother to hand over the ring, to rough him up a little if he refused.

He had not sent them to torture Albrecht to death while failing to find the ring. He had sent them to find Charles Gibson at the Hotel Sospiri. He had not sent them to make a scene, threaten staff, get captured on CCTV and come to the attention of the police.

For all its cosmopolitan atmosphere, the streets of Istanbul were not full of large, badly behaved African men. The Mogadishans had become a liability—a liability that could have led to the capture of Hans Peter von Seidel, allegedly deceased.

The steel-grey waters of the Mediterranean moved restlessly before him mirroring his mood. It was Wiesenthal's fault of course that he was in such a desperate situation, Wiesenthal and the girl—the spoiled little rich girl whom he had rescued and who had eventually betrayed him. Life had been good in Argentina for almost thirty years.

His wealth, judiciously 'acquired'—and even more judiciously banked—over the war years had enabled him to buy a large estate to the north of Buenos Aires. In the early years, there had been plenty people prepared to turn a blind eye to inconsistencies in the life stories of wealthy men in return for a suitable 'consideration'.

His two bodyguards had served with him throughout the war; his protection and their own culpability in war crimes had guaranteed unquestioning loyalty. All three men had false Dutch passports, his in the name of Pieter Steen—an identity he had comfortably grown into until a day in 1987 when it had threatened his very freedom. By the early 1960s, the years of glittering balls and lavish dinners were over.

Simon Wiesenthal's obsessive search in Argentina for Martin Bormann (who, it later transpired, had actually committed suicide in Berlin in 1945) and fellow Nazis meant that he had had to live a more reclusive and circumspect life, keeping well out of the public eye.

His circle of associates had narrowed to men with a war-time past to hide; and in 1972, his bodyguards and only trusted friends had died within weeks of each other—one of a lymphoma and the other in a stupid bar brawl over a woman. They had been replaced by locals whose loyalty stretched only as far as Hans Peter's capacity to pay.

It was about this time that the nightmares had started, when ghosts from the past returned to accuse or seek revenge; when his eight year old brother, Hans Jurgen, came to ask why he had left him locked in a barn in sub-zero temperatures precipitating the pneumonia which killed him three days later.

In 1982, while seeking fleeting solace in the arms of one of Rosa's girls in 'The Red Peony', a discreet bordello in Pergamino, he had been struck by the classic poise and beauty of a 'new girl'. Nineteen-year-old Maria Silvia Martinez was the daughter of a commander in the armed forces and close associate of General Gualtieri, the Argentinian president.

On her fourth arrest, this time for driving under the influence of alcohol and cocaine, no one from her father's household came to collect her. Repeated telephone calls to her home met with the same response from the butler, "General Martinez wishes to inform you that Maria Silvia Martinez no longer resides at this address."

Thrown out onto the street with nowhere to go and her bank account blocked, she had been trying unsuccessfully to beg when one of Rosa's scouts had spotted her. Hans Peter had simply bought her from Rosa at an eye-watering price. Five years later, she would escape and betray him, but it was partly his own doing; his own fault for loving her to the detriment of his judgement.

He had known she was lonely and bored, cooped up on a remote estate with no company of her own age. The only variation in her otherwise stultifying routine had been solitary rides on horseback across the estate or occasional visits to Pergamino to buy clothes, accompanied by an ever-watchful driver. The only visitors to the house were anxious, old men debating behind closed doors whether the time had come to leave Argentina.

Thus, it was that in 1985, he had given her permission to attend a course at the local university with the stipulation that she would be accompanied at all times by the driver, and should not fraternise with other students outside class.

He could not have anticipated that the driver would take such a relaxed approach to his supervisory duties, or that Maria Silvia would strike up a close friendship with a young Dutch student, Jan-Marten, with whom she would spend every break.

Chapter 13
Maria Silvia Martinez:
Pergamino, 1985–1987

Although, Maria Silvia spoke Spanish with Hans Peter (Pieter to her), she had picked up quite a lot of what she assumed was Dutch from listening to his conversations with visitors. One day in the university cafe, she thought she would surprise Jan-Marten by saying something to him in his own language. He looked puzzled for a moment then smiled and said, "I'm sorry, I don't understand German."

"But that was Dutch!" She replied, "It's what I hear at home." They looked at each other for a long moment as realisation dawned. It was common knowledge that many Nazis with a past to bury had sought refuge in South America after the war and Pieter Steen matched the profile.

That evening, she had been left alone in the house while Hans Peter went to a meeting. Unusually, he had left his study door unlocked and, with fumbling fingers and a piece of wire, she had worked at the locks on his desk—a skill she had developed in her cocaine years searching her father's desk for money. The lower drawer on the left-hand side appeared shallower than that on the right and a sharp tap indicated the presence of a false base.

Concealed in the cavity, she found a number of documents all written in German cursive script, and a Waffen SS military ID in the name of Hans Peter von Seidel. Checking that she was still alone, she risked calling Jan-Marten.

"What can you find out about an SS Ober Gruppen Führer called Hans Peter von Seidel? We can't see each other tomorrow because it's Saturday and Pieter knows we have no classes, but I'll call you when the coast is clear; this can't wait till Monday!"

"Will do, but be very, very careful," he said.

She did not see Pieter till lunch time the following day. He entered the dining room and announced he was going out without staying to eat. "When will you be back?" She asked.

"What business is that of yours?" He replied curtly. Was it just her imagination, or did he suspect something? She had been careful to put everything in the study back the way she had found it, but had she missed something? She couldn't eat, couldn't sit still, couldn't control her jangling nerves.

She had to know the identity of the man she had lived with for the past five years. It seemed an eternity before she heard his car rolling out of the garage and down the drive. When she was sure he had left the estate, she went to the phone checking that none of the household staff was nearby.

Her hands were trembling so violently, she had to redial after hitting a wrong number at the first attempt. Jan-Marten responded immediately, sounding tense. "I have just got back from the library, and yes, I have found something—found more than you would ever want to know." As he spoke, she felt herself grow cold, unable to control the tremor in her legs.

Jan-Marten had a lot to tell her, all of it horrifying. He had just begun telling her about Hans Peter's involvement in the massacre at Sant Anna di Stazzema when she became aware of a presence behind her and the receiver was removed from her grasp and gently replaced in the cradle. It all happened so fast, she didn't even have time to cry out before Hans Peter struck her hard sending her reeling across the room.

Before she regained her balance, he was hitting her again with a savagery fuelled by fear and a sense of betrayal. Finally, crumpled on the floor in a mist of pain, she heard him shout, "Take her up to her room and lock her in until I decide what to do with her!"

More than two hours passed before the pain had receded sufficiently to enable her to think. She had bruises all over her body and her lips were split, but miraculously no bones were broken. No one came for her. She heard the car leaving in the late afternoon and it hadn't returned by the time she fell into a troubled sleep in the early hours of the morning. A deathly silence seemed to pervade the house and grounds.

The guard let her out twice to go to the bathroom and a desperate plan began to form in her mind. Towards dawn, she woke the sleeping guard and asked to go to the bathroom once more. Inside, she locked the door, pulled the flush then turned on the shower full blast. She opened the window. With some difficulty, she managed to squeeze herself out and reached for a down pipe.

As she transferred her weight from the window sill to the pipe, it detached from the wall sending a metal fixture tumbling to the ground with a sickening clang. Terrified, she waited for sounds of movement but none came and she let herself slide down to the ground and walked silently to the stables.

Petrified and with pain racking her damaged body, Maria Silvia buried her face in the soft, smooth neck of her horse drawing comfort from her warmth and her smell. Silke was surprised and delighted to see her mistress so early in the morning but, with an animal's intuition, sensed that this was no ordinary morning.

Maria Silvia winced at the noise every time Silke's hooves made contact with the stone flags paving the yard as they made their cautious way towards the bridle path. No sound came from the house and they rode at a gallop to the boundary of the estate where it bordered onto a country road. Recently, a car driven by a young joy rider had careered off the road ending up embedded in the boundary wall.

The wall had withstood the impact reasonably well, but at the point of impact some dislodged stones offered useful foot holds for an inexpert climber like Maria Silvia. It broke her heart to leave Silke but there was no way the horse could clear the wall and going out by a gate would have risked immediate discovery. Besides, how could she look after her with no food or stabling to offer?

Maria Silvia was tempted to tether Silke in case she ran back to the house and raised the alarm too soon, but in the end decided to leave her free. She would never know that Silke had waited for her until it was almost nightfall when an estate worker found her on his way home.

Maria Silvia half walked half ran along the road putting as much distance as possible between herself and anyone searching for her, and trying unsuccessfully to hitch a lift from the few cars passing along the road. She had almost given up hope when an old truck, driven by an even older man pulled up. The driver took one look at her bruised face and told her to jump in.

"Where are you going?" He asked.

"Anywhere far away from here," she replied.

"Did your husband do that to you?"

"No, someone else, it's a long story."

"Is that someone likely to be following you?" The driver asked, suddenly aware of the possible consequences of his impetuous offer of help.

"Probably," she said, "but if he catches us, I'll tell him I held you at knife point—if you have a knife I can use to convince him, that is."

"Well, I am going to Cordoba and can drop you off anywhere on the way if that suits."

"Cordoba will be fine."

"I hope you don't mind roughing it then, I sleep in the cab."

"Rougher things have happened to me recently," she said with an attempt at a smile, swiftly regretting it as her swollen lips registered their protest.

She would phone Jan-Marten from Cordoba. He would know where she should go and whom she needed to tell.

Twenty-four hours earlier, Jan-Marten had stared at the receiver as the line went dead. What had happened? Had someone come into the room while Maria Silvia was on the phone; had Hans Peter suspected that something was up and returned to the house?

He was suddenly filled with an awful sense of foreboding—a man who had thought nothing of participating in the massacre of thousands would not hesitate to murder a young woman who could at any moment expose his identity and destroy his life. He had no way of contacting Maria Silvia; to phone back could place her in even greater danger. He didn't even know where she lived.

Should he go to the police with what he knew? But what good would that do? The local police would have to pass something as serious as the exposure of a high profile war criminal to some much higher authority and that would take time, too much time. And what else did he have to report— that a girl he was fond of but who lived with a wealthy older man had hung up on him.

He could imagine the laughter. "So Sugar Daddy turned up just as the two of you were having a nice little chat…"

It was time to talk to his father and tell him everything. His father would know what to do.

Hans Peter knew he should have killed her immediately. He should have beaten her until she revealed the name of the man on the other end of the line, then killed her. But he couldn't do it because in spite of everything he still loved her. She was the only person he had ever loved.

He sank onto a sofa, overwhelmed by waves of grief, fear and despair. If he let her live, she would tell. A different kind of woman might just have held the threat of exposure over his head for the rest of his life, but Maria Silvia was not that kind of woman. So, for now she was locked in her room but he couldn't keep her there forever. He would have to silence her.

He needed space to think. He couldn't remain under the same roof as Maria Silvia knowing what he had to do, and he had to plan the best way to dispose of her without arousing the suspicions of staff. Fortunately, the next day was Sunday. Yes, he would do it on Sunday when the housekeeper and cook had the day off, although he knew he was simply postponing the inevitable.

He got into his car and drove for 200 kilometres until he reached the outskirts of Buenos Aires and a discreet, four star hotel near the stud farm where he bought his horses. He checked in for two nights requesting that dinner be brought to his room that evening but booking dinner in the restaurant for the following evening.

"Welcome back, Sir," said the cheery girl on the reception desk.

"Thank you, I'm thinking about buying another horse. I'll have a look at what's on offer tomorrow and think about it overnight."

His alibi established, all he had to do was plan the next day. He would set off for home early, apologise to Maria Silvia and tell her that he would take her to their favourite beauty spot beside one of the many rivers feeding the Rio de la Plata so that they could talk in peace, then go for a leisurely lunch. He would do it there and let the river and the piranha fish destroy all trace of her.

With any luck, he would be back in Buenos Aires in time to consolidate his alibi, visiting the stud farm and dining at the hotel. The only person who would know he had returned to the house was the guard and there were a number of ways in which his silence could be assured—none of which would cause him the kind of pain killing Maria Silvia would.

He had arrived back home to be greeted by an eerie silence. There was no sign of the guard, Maria Silvia's bedroom door was unlocked and there was no sign of Maria Silvia either. The bathroom door had been forced, the window was open and the downpipe was detached from the wall. It required little imagination to work out the chain of events.

Preferring to avoid the wrath of his employer, the guard had made himself permanently scarce, the loss of employment being infinitely preferable to the loss of his life. Maria Silvia's horse was missing too. How far could she have gone on horseback…and in which direction?

He wasn't to know that at that very moment, Maria Silvia was in a trucker's cafe 150 kilometres away waiting while her new companion finished a hasty breakfast and refuelled his truck. What he did know was that she had enough time to report what she knew and that Argentina was no longer a safe place. He would have to leave, probably for some failed state in Africa where he could lie low for a while.

How much money could he raise immediately without arousing suspicion? What would happen to his estate? Would his bank accounts be blocked? It was Germany in 1945 all over again, only this time he was sixty-seven years old, not twenty-seven.

Chapter 14
Edinburgh, November 1995

Anya was relieved to see that she was not the sole representative of her generation at the youth hostel. A few grey-haired travellers lingered in the café putting off the moment when they would have to face the elements and get down to the serious business of sightseeing across a grey and wind-swept Edinburgh.

Stuffing a roll and an apple in her back pack, Anya set off for the Public Library on George IV Bridge. Even on a cold, dark winter morning, her first glimpse of Edinburgh Castle almost took her breath away.

Towering over Princes Street and the Gardens below, its forbidding cliffs and mighty walls said all that needed to be said about the folly of attempting an attack—a warning that successive waves of would-be assailants had ignored at their peril.

It wasn't a beautiful castle like so many in the gentler lands further south, but as a symbol of raw power and witness to a thousand years of turbulent Scottish history, it more than made up in dramatic impact for any lack in architectural finesse.

A kindly librarian asked if she could help.

"I am looking for Edinburgh telephone directories for 1991 and 1992 if you have these," Anya replied.

"I'm afraid not; your best recourse would probably be to contact British Telecom directly."

Anya sat down heavily, faced with the daunting prospect of explaining her request to some bemused call centre operator on the Indian sub-continent who would 'certainly be glad to help you, Ma'am, only he or she would not have a clue about how to penetrate the complex bureaucratic tangle that might eventually lead to someone who knew how to access an old phone book.

Not for the first time since her life had fallen apart, Anya realised just how easily she was discouraged by difficulty these days. Noticing her disappointment, the librarian approached her.

"I've just had an idea," she said. "My mother is a hoarder and I think I have seen a pile of old phonebooks on a shelf under her telephone table. I usually call in on her at lunchtimes and could check for you. If she has the years you are interested in, I could bring these back with me after lunch."

True to her word, the librarian appeared at one pm with an armful of directories for 1991, 1992 and 1993. Anya decided to start with 1992. It was slow going and the tiny print had started to jump before her tired, sleep-deprived eyes when she found it.

Gibson *Dr C. E. 11, Bellevue Avenue 0131 556 9929.*

Could it possibly be…? Her mind raced back to the news coverage of the murder of an Edinburgh academic called

Gibson...Christopher Gibson? No, a shorter name...Charles Gibson? The case she had irrationally come to think of as having significance for her.

She looked at her watch, four pm. She handed back the phonebooks, thanking the librarian profusely and left heading for town and the map of the city centre she had noticed on the wall of the hostel. The Bellevue area was at the very eastern edge of the Georgian New Town.

A row of substantial early Victorian town houses flanked one side of Bellevue Avenue and a line of large trees partially obscured a high wall running along the other side, ending in a horse-shoe-shaped cul de sac. Number 11 was the last house in the row with large, corner windows overlooking a small garden. There were no lights on at the front of the house although darkness had already fallen.

Hesitantly, she opened the wrought iron gate, walked up the short path and rang the doorbell. There was no response. As she left, she saw a young woman walking along the avenue pushing a buggy laden with toddler, shopping and a school bag belonging to the little girl skipping along beside her. The woman pulled level just as Anya was exiting the gate, eyeing her with suspicion.

"Can I help you?" She asked anxiously.

"I am trying to trace the owner of a valuable object that has come into my possession, and the only clue I have is a phone number found with it. The number belonged to a Dr Gibson who, I believe, once lived at this address. I was hoping that someone here might know how I could get in touch with relatives of Dr Gibson."

The woman looked visibly shaken. "I...I can't help you...not just now...not with the children. Can you come back when my husband gets home?…Yes, that would be best. I can't talk just now, not with the children, not on my own…Excuse me." With that, she pushed past Anya, frantically searching for her keys and dropping her handbag in the process.

Anya retrieved it and asked as gently as she could, "What time might I call after your husband gets home?"

"Seven pm, the children will be in bed by then." With that, the woman disappeared through the front door and closed it firmly. Anya heard the unmistakable sound of a bolt sliding across.

Anya stared after her for a moment, before turning away. She felt really bad about frightening the woman, but even if mention of the house's previous owner was unwelcome, it surely didn't merit such an extreme reaction. Re-joining the main road back into town, she stopped to admire the beautiful Playfair Church of St Mary Bellevue.

The clock on the bell tower showed that it was already five-fifteen pm. Further up the road, she noticed a welcoming pub, 'The Cask and Barrel', and on impulse decided to escape the biting wind and wait there until seven pm. Inside the pub, a lively crowd of people were celebrating the end of the working day while others watched a football match playing on a large screen.

It was warm and sufficiently anonymous for her to feel quite comfortable huddled in a corner trying to make a coffee last as long as possible and, to her surprise, she got so caught up in the excitement of the football match that she almost lost track of the time.

At seven o'clock, she reluctantly left the warmth of the pub and made her way back to Bellevue Avenue. This time, lights shone in the front room of number 11 and the door was promptly opened by a stocky man in his thirties with a shock of red hair and pale freckled skin. He ushered her in, introducing himself as Peter Bruce as he took her coat.

"You have met my wife, Rosemary, already I believe," he said as he showed Anya into the living room. Rosemary jumped to her feet and began a stammering apology for her earlier behaviour before being cut short by her husband who was intent on introducing a third person standing beside the marble fireplace.

A tall, well-built man in his late fifties strode across the room, hand outstretched. "John Arbuthnot," he said. "I apologise for the intrusion, but I am the chief inspector in charge of the Gibson case." Anya suddenly felt faint, she hadn't been expecting this. She knew it was silly, she had nothing to fear from this policeman, but her interrogation over Amir had left its indelible mark.

Sensing her unease, Arbuthnot hastened to reassure her, "Why don't you have a seat and I'll explain why I am here. There is nothing to worry about. I am clutching at straws in a case that has offered nothing but dead ends so far. Peter and Rosemary know that if anything turns up that might provide a new lead in the Gibson case, I should be informed immediately."

"From all accounts, Dr Gibson was a highly respected, kindly man and I want to put whoever was responsible for his brutal murder behind bars for a very long time. It is a case that almost certainly has links with the earlier murder of a close friend of Dr Gibson's in Istanbul, leaving the Turkish police as baffled as we are. It would be very helpful, therefore, if you could tell us what led you to this address; and Rosemary mentioned something about a valuable object."

Anya sat on the edge of the chair and began to tell the story.

"It started with the coat Mr Bruce has just hung up in the hall. I bought it in the Oxfam shop in Southend-on-Sea and when I got it home, I discovered a strange gold ring caught in the lining and a card with a telephone number on it in a pocket."

"The phone number was discontinued and staff at the Oxfam shop did not have a record of the donor, so I decided to come to Edinburgh to try to find an address where someone might be able to help me trace the original owner of the coat and ring. A helpful member of staff in the Central Library managed to get hold of old phonebooks for me and I traced the telephone number to this address. That's all, really."

"Could it be the very same coat?" Peter asked excitedly. "As John knows, we bought this house for a fraction of its value because of what happened here. Once Dr Gibson's estate had been settled, his lawyer sent in a house clearance company to empty the place, but they overlooked a pile of coats and boots in the utility room at the back door."

"When we moved in, I bundled these into a bin bag and took them to the Oxfam shop in Morningside Road; I teach English at a school near there. There was an almost new coat just like yours among them."

"It could have belonged to Dr Gibson's mother," said John thoughtfully. "Sadly, towards the end of her life, she suffered from dementia and had taken to wandering and getting lost which could explain the telephone number in the pocket. It doesn't explain how a coat left in an Oxfam shop in Edinburgh could have ended up in Southend-on-Sea though."

"Don't charity shops sometimes send donations to other shops where they might sell better?" Rosemary said, her anxiety abating in the intrigue of the moment. "Though I suppose the Morningside Road shop must be one of the best places to sell an expensive coat. I don't know much about Southend."

"Tell us about the ring," John said. Anya undid the top button of her blouse and extracted a solid gold chain—a gift from Amir—briefly if reluctantly restored to service to transport the heavy ring in safety. They all stared at the ring wordlessly.

Rosemary broke the silence. "It's hideous, but somehow powerfully malignant," she whispered; her impulsive reaction expressing the impact of the ring perfectly.

"This might just be the break we are looking for," John said, almost in a whisper. "We have always assumed that Dr Gibson and his friend, Monsignor von Seidel, were in possession of an item of value or information that the murderers were after. Although, their rooms were ransacked, money and valuables were left untouched ruling out common burglary as a motive."

"If Dr Gibson had wanted to hide a valuable ring, given to him in trust by his friend, what better place to conceal it than inside the lining of his mother's coat?"

"Thank you everyone for your help this evening, but I need to get back to the station now. Can you come with me, Miss Wilson?" Noticing her panic, he smiled and added, "It is your ring, but I would like our forensics experts to have a look at it and get some photographs and impressions taken."

There was nothing Anya could do, but go along with this and she was left for about an hour nursing a cup of tea and a rumbling stomach in a waiting room at the police station in Gayfield Square. Finally, John Arbuthnot reappeared with her ring and suggested she replace it on the chain.

"Will you at least let me take you for a meal, given the inconvenience we have caused you?" The last thing Anya wanted to do, was to prolong her evening in the company of this policeman, but she was in a strange town, poor and very hungry, so the answer was yes. "Before we go, there is something I need to say to you." Arbuthnot drew up a metal chair and sat facing her.

"We are dealing with very dangerous criminals who will stop at nothing to get whatever it is they are looking for. I more than half suspect this ring may be it. Now, in all likelihood, the trail to Dr Gibson's property has gone cold as far as the criminals are concerned."

"If they had wanted to return to rip up the floorboards or look out for a visitor who might know something useful, they would have done so while the property was empty. I very much doubt that they will be watching the property now that the Bruce family has moved in, although Rosemary lives in constant fear that they will come back. It was her husband's idea to buy the place, but she clearly hates being there."

"In short, it is highly unlikely that anyone has been following you or watching the house this evening, but we cannot take chances with your safety, so first of all, I am going to leave the ring with you for now; you are safer with it than without it. You must promise me that if anyone asks for it, you will give it to them immediately. I have seen what they do to people who do not cooperate."

"Secondly, you cannot go back to the youth hostel; it is too difficult to secure with so many people coming and going. We have arranged for you to stay at a small guest house we use, and there will be a WPC on duty overnight."

"Tomorrow, I would like you to accompany me to the Oxfam shop and to Dr Gibson's lawyer in the morning and I have arranged for us to visit an expert on antique gold to see what he makes of the ring. I am sorry to commandeer your holiday in this way, but we need your help."

Anya sat in stunned silence as once again her life seemed to be racing out of her control then, recovering her senses, she blurted, "I can't afford to stay in a guest house and my bus ticket is for tomorrow morning and I can't change it. Thank you, but I need to leave things as they are and..."

"The room is paid for, and we'll sort out a train ticket for you when you are ready to go home."

Did she have the right to refuse? She supposed she was now 'helping police with their inquiries'. In spite of herself, she was beginning to find the prospect of sleuthing tomorrow decidedly more attractive than sitting on a bus for ten hours.

Arbuthnot took her to a small Italian restaurant nearby where he was clearly well known. She happily accepted the owner's recommendation of stuffed zucchini flowers followed by a delicious linguine marinara. Half a litre of the house red helped conversation to flow and she learned that John Arbuthnot had been born and raised on the Black Isle in the north of Scotland.

He had studied criminology in London, married a fellow student and joined the Met on graduation. The marriage hadn't lasted, but he had a daughter and grandchildren in London and a sister in Canada. Eight years ago, he had transferred to Edinburgh to be nearer his increasingly frail parents in their final years. He was determined to solve the Gibson case before he retired in three months' time.

"There are some cases that won't let you go until you have solved them," he explained. "And this is one of them."

Arbuthnot seemed to hesitate. "Do you mind if I ask what happened to you," he said, quickly following up with, "I apologise, I have no right to ask that. A policeman's fault, we never know when to stop asking questions!"

Anya smiled, not much wrong with this policeman's intuition, she thought.

"I don't mind. I was a diplomat at the British Embassy in Rome when I fell in love with the wrong man; he couldn't have been more wrong. He led a double life, working under cover for the Iranian Intelligence Services and I fell for a classic case of entrapment. It cost me my job, could have landed me with a charge of treason."

"The reference provided by my former ambassador would scarcely qualify me for a job in a gangland laundry. The first two paragraphs of the reference were fairly standard, but the final paragraph left little to encourage a prospective employer." Every word of it is indelibly etched on my mind:

*However, we had no option but to terminate Miss Wilson's employment with the Foreign and Commonwealth Office. In an unforgiveable error of judgement, she allowed herself to be entrapped by a member of the **intelligence agency** of a hostile state, posing as an Italian doctor. She failed to carry out due diligence to check his identity.*

Furthermore, she allowed this man to reside in embassy property without seeking clearance, and gave him access to her official laptop computer. I therefore could not recommend Miss Wilson for any post that required good judgement; or for any post that involved the handling of confidential material.

"All I will add is that the man concerned was a highly respected consultant oncologist at a famous children's hospital in Rome and he had Italian citizenship. However, ignorance of his real identity is no defence. The CIA had been watching him for some time and got very edgy when he entered into a relationship with me."

"The ambassador might have stressed that an internal investigation did not find any evidence of sensitive information passing between us, but he was understandably in revenge mode when he wrote the reference. It cost me the job I had been offered as PA to the Director of a Pharmaceutical company—the only serious job I have got anywhere near since I was sacked."

"The director was kind enough to copy the reference to me as he felt I might wish to challenge the final paragraph before applying for another job. He regretted that his Trustees would not allow him to appoint me because of the sensitive nature of their research into new drugs. I have not challenged the reference because it is factually accurate, although the 'spin' is malicious. Hence, my current impoverished state."

Arbuthnot listened in companionable silence. "That's quite a story," he said eventually. "Thank you for telling me." Years of watching body language and listening to stories told him that he was hearing the truth. He also sensed the deep hurt underlying the matter-of-fact delivery of the account he had just heard. This was an interesting woman and for some reason, he felt a sudden desire to protect her.

"What happened to the doctor?"

"The Iranians sprung him from the hospital and put him on a plane to Teheran before the CIA got to him. I have no idea what has happened to him since, but I subsequently heard that his family is well connected with the regime so perhaps he has survived."

A WPC stood inside the front door of a pretty little guest house tucked away on a quiet street in Edinburgh's fashionable West End. The owner, a friendly middle-aged woman with grey hair pulled back into a tight coil at the nape of her neck, showed her to her room, asked if she needed anything and wished her goodnight. It was almost midnight. She looked around the room in amused disbelief.

Instead of bedding down hungry in a spartan hostel cubicle, she had dined well and was now surveying a large, inviting double bed, matching textiles throughout the room and comfortable occasional furniture. A modern bathroom sported a range of Ortigia toiletries and thick white towels. That night she slept dreamlessly until she was woken by a polite tap on the door and a reminder that breakfast would be served at eight-thirty am.

Chapter 15
Police Station,
Gayfield Square, Edinburgh

Early next morning, John Arbuthnot received some promising news about the ring. Magdalena von Seidel had rung him first thing to say that the ring in the photo he had faxed to her was very like a 'vulgar contraption' her grandfather used to wear, but she could not be 100% sure. Her grandfather had not been in the habit of letting her close enough to study anything he wore!

She would take the photo to her mother at the weekend. Hanna might have a clearer memory of Hans Ludvig's ring. "I should go to see her anyway. She is not getting any younger!"

"And how is the Baroness?" Arbuthnot had asked Magdalena remembering with affection the feisty woman he had met early in the investigation.

"Still adamantly *Frau Brandt,* not the Dowager Baroness von Seidel, still living in her old, cold flat in Berlin; still steadfastly resistant to all forms of technological advance so there is no point in emailing her; still refusing to spend money; still preparing for the next outbreak of war; and still developing bizarre theories about the murders—mostly involving a resurrected Hans Peter. In fact, barely changed from the last time you met her." Arbuthnot had laughed.

"It's a while since I heard from her."

"I fear Chief Inspector Demercol has been less fortunate; she calls him regularly."

"Perhaps I lack his patrician charm."

"Perhaps you lack focus on her beloved Albrecht—Charles' fate is very much secondary in my mother's campaign!"

"She is a force to be reckoned with, that's for sure!"

"I tell you what. If you find the killer, save everyone the trouble and expense of lengthy trials and imprisonment, just lock him in a room with my mother and a cricket bat."

Arbuthnot had smiled as he replaced the receiver. The von Seidel women, mother and daughter, were something else. He looked forward to contacting the Baroness again to discuss the provenance of the ring.

His early meeting with Chief Superintendent Markham had been less positive.

"I know how much this case means to you, John, and finding this ring may help solve the puzzle of what the killers were looking for. What it doesn't do is tell us why they were so desperate to lay hands on it, or help us identify them…unless you were thinking of flushing them out by telling the press we have had a major breakthrough."

"And all that would do would be to encourage the killers to abduct some poor soul as hostage, or threaten to set off a bomb in a public place in an attempt to force us to hand over the ring. I can let you have a few more days to look into this further, but I can't go to the chief constable to ask for more resources based on what you have at the moment."

"I would like to find out more about the significance of the ring before deciding what to do next."

"Very well. Keep me informed." With that, the meeting was over and Arbuthnot grabbed his coat and left the building.

Edinburgh Day 2: The Ring

He found Anya relaxing in the guest house dining room reading *The Scotsman.* He ordered two coffees and talked through the plans for the day.

"We'll call at the Oxfam shop first thing, then I have arranged to see Charles Gibson's lawyer at eleven. After that, we have a bit of a break I'm afraid. I want to take the ring to Niall Chambers, an expert on antique gold, to see what he makes of it. Our forensics experts think the ring has been heavily re-modelled at some time but can't tell much more than that."

"We need Niall's expertise. Unfortunately, he is having treatment for cancer at the moment but says there is a short window in the day when he doesn't feel too bad and suggests we call at his house at four-thirty pm."

Doing a rapid time calculation in her head, Anya said, "That may not leave me enough time to get back to Southend by train this evening…although, I suppose I could catch the overnight bus to London…"

"If you are free to stay another night in Edinburgh, I can easily sort that out with the guest house."

"Are you sure? I don't know that I am being much help to the police."

"Let me be the judge of that, Miss Wilson."

"Anya, please."

The Oxfam shop in Morningside was bright and cheerful, its elegantly dressed window clearly indicating that it served the upper end of charity shop clientele. A charming assistant listened thoughtfully to their query then pursed her lips in an obvious sign of regret.

"We might be able to trace the donor of a high value item like your coat, but it's much less likely that we will be able to trace the purchaser, not if the sale took place over twelve months ago. Most of our customers pay in cash. The manager will be in at mid-day. I could ask if she remembers anything. She has worked in this shop for years."

Arbuthnot said they would call back at one pm and they headed for the lawyer's office. Entering the elegant chambers on Heriot Row, Arbuthnot wondered, not for the first time, whether he had chosen the right career path thirty-five years ago. John Adam was a slight man in his early seventies.

His pin stripe suit looked as if it had been purchased when he had been of heavier, more robust proportions, but his generally dishevelled air belied a bright intelligence and he welcomed the policeman he had met several times following Charles Gibson's death with genuine warmth.

"I have looked out the inventory for Charles Gibson's estate, John, and there is no reference to a ring and, as you know, there were no valuable items missing when we checked the house contents against the inventory. If Charles possessed this ring, for some reason he chose not to include it on the list of his valuable possessions."

It had been a frustrating morning, but there was some good news waiting for them back at the station. Forensics had managed to lift two sets of prints from the card with the telephone number, Dr Gibson's and Anya's, confirming the connection between the coat and the murdered man.

Better news awaited them at the Oxfam shop. The manager remembered selling the coat to an elderly lady who had seemed rather confused and reluctant to make the purchase. She had argued with her daughter and refused to allow the daughter to pay, taking a perverse delight in being 'forced' to spend more than she could afford on a coat she didn't want.

The daughter was so embarrassed by the scene that she made a generous gift-aid donation—her name was Catherine Stewart and she lives in Lauder Road.

A housekeeper answered the phone and said that Dr Stewart was expected home by three pm.

John took Anya for a quick lunch in the 'Canny Man', a popular, historic tavern on Morningside Road. They chose a quiet table in a small, panelled room at the rear of the bar and puzzled over how the coat might have made its way from Edinburgh to the south of England. As they set off for the short journey to Lauder Road, they hoped Catherine Stewart might be able to shed light on the mystery.

Catherine Stewart, née Mitchell, lived in an enormous house with a pillared entrance. They were shown into a large drawing room furnished in the clinically elegant style typically found on the front cover of magazines like *Ideal Home*. The housekeeper brought in coffee, served in exquisite, gold-rimmed china, and left them in peace.

Catherine Stewart had none of the airs and graces Arbuthnot associated with Edinburgh's super-rich. She taught history at the University of Edinburgh—an idiosyncrasy her mother-in-law struggled to understand, but at least it wasn't a career that undermined the standing of her financier husband in the eyes of those whose opinions mattered in Edinburgh. She winced as she recalled the purchase of the coat.

"I was brought up by my aunt who lived in Leigh-on-Sea in Essex, and the coat was for her. She had come to spend Christmas with us as she usually did but arrived without any warm clothes. I had not realised how confused she had become in the four months since I had seen her last. Anyway, we had a bit of a row over the coat."

"She had flatly refused to buy a new one, so Oxfam was the compromise. I found an almost new coat at £50—much like the one you are wearing, but Aunt Agnes made an almighty fuss over buying it then complained that it hurt her legs when she wore it. It went into the back of her wardrobe when she got home and I don't think she ever wore it again."

"Aunt Agnes died in April this year, but it was September before I got round to clearing out the house. It had been my childhood home and I found it difficult to let it go. I left her coat along with a few other things at the Oxfam shop in Southend-on-Sea. I don't know if that helps you at all."

"You have been very helpful indeed, Dr Stewart," Arbuthnot reassured her, barely able to suppress his excitement. "You have solved the mystery of how the coat made its way from Edinburgh to the south of England for us. Thank you very much for your time, and for the welcome coffee, but we should be on our way now and leave you to get on with your day."

"It was a pleasure. I spend my life researching historical mysteries and it has been a fascinating experience providing a tiny piece of evidence that might solve a modern mystery! I am glad to have been able to help, and good luck with the investigation! I knew Charles Gibson, we were colleagues at Edinburgh."

"He was a delightful, gentle man who wore his learning lightly. What happened to him was unspeakably awful."

As they left Lauder Road heading for Niall Chambers' home in Polwarth Terrace, Arbuthnot felt more hopeful than he had done in months. They had a ring which connected the deaths of Albrecht von Seidel and his friend, Charles Gibson. It was a strange looking object but could have been what the killers were looking for.

Possession of the ring had apparently made both men anxious, if contemporary accounts of their states of mind were to be believed, and Dr Gibson had felt the need to hide the ring in an obscure place. Two good men had died for that ring, and John Arbuthnot was determined to find out why.

Edinburgh: Polwarth Terrace

"Well, if it isn't John Arbuthnot, intent, no doubt, on disturbing an old man's peaceful convalescence! But why am I keeping you at the door, come in, come in!"

The man who greeted Arbuthnot with such obvious warmth was slightly built. A knitted cardigan several sizes too large for him fell in folds over a pair of equally baggy flannels. A few tight silver curls ringed his head defying the effects of the chemotherapy drugs coursing through his veins. Bright, intelligent eyes and an engaging smile shone through the grey pallor of cancer.

"Now, young lady, you must be Miss Wilson and I'm sorry to find you in such questionable company, but never fear, I shall keep you safe from this man!"

Anya found herself smiling broadly as she shook Niall's fragile hand. The drawing room they entered could not have been more different from the austere elegance of Catherine Stewart's. Books lined the walls and lay in piles on the floor. Venerable sofas were covered with textiles from the four corners of the Earth.

A Bechstein grand piano dominated one corner of the room and a large cat occupied pride of place before a wood burning stove. Framed photographs of friends and family jostled for space on every available surface with intricately carved inlaid boxes, oriental lamps, delicate porcelain vases, car keys and pens.

This room was as warm and welcoming as their host. As soon as they were settled with a large sherry apiece, Niall got straight to the point, "So, let me see this ring that you have found." Anya slipped it off the chain.

Niall rolled the ring over and over peering closely at it through a jeweller's magnifying glass.

"Good heavens! I have never seen anything like this, where on Earth did you find it? A fine gentleman's signet ring and a fascinating inset have suffered a terrible fate together!"

"What can you tell us about it, Niall?" Arbuthnot asked with just a hint of impatience in his voice.

"Well, where to start? Two very fine pieces have been heavily re-modelled to create this monstrous ring. The thing that puzzles me is that this is the work of a very fine craftsman. However, I cannot imagine any goldsmith of this ability committing such an act of vandalism unless he had a gun at his head."

What Niall did not know was just how precisely he had described the experience of a terrified Jewish goldsmith in Hamburg in 1936.

"The original ring dates from the late nineteenth century and started out its life as a gentleman's signet ring—German judging by the markings. If you look through this glass, you can just make out the mark of the Sachs Goldwaren Fabrik, one of the best-known goldsmiths in Germany in the late nineteenth and early twentieth centuries."

"The owners were Jewish and their studio in Hamburg was destroyed in 1938 along with thousands of other Jewish-owned businesses during the Kristallnacht riots. The inset, on the other hand, is Middle Eastern in origin and very much older than the ring itself, just look at the magnificent detail. The craftsmanship is exquisite."

"It looks like the decoration from a ceremonial weapon of some sort, possibly the hilt of a sword or dagger. It could be Turkish or Persian, but you would need to get expert advice on this. The heavy mount has been added more recently to house the inset which is much larger than the original face of the ring would have been."

"Whoever re-modelled the ring did an excellent job of matching the gold of the original ring with the newer mount, but the gold of the inset is different and the inset is probably three or four hundred years old. I know that the Byzantines used to use heavily embossed rings as proof of identity and as seals for documents, but my guess is that this inset is from the later Turkish/Ottoman period."

"We need to get this looked at by an expert on Ottoman and Persian antiquities and I know just the man—my old friend, Dr Faisal Arslan at the Museum of Turkish and Islamic Arts in Istanbul."

"If you could alert him to our interest, we can send photos and ask for an opinion," said Arbuthnot.

"Good heavens, no. For something like this, an expert must have the artefact in his own hands, be able to study it under magnification and compare it with records of similar pieces."

"Isn't there an expert nearer at hand, then? What about a curator at the V&A for example?"

An impish, slightly guilty smile spread across Niall's face. "It's just so long since I was last in Istanbul and I would love to see it one more time before I depart this life—and Faisal Arslan is, without doubt, the best man for this!"

Anya and John Arbuthnot stared at each other in astonishment, not knowing how to respond to this. There had been no thought of involving Niall beyond this initial meeting let alone suggesting he travel to Istanbul.

"Niall, my superintendent would have a seizure if I suggested travelling to Istanbul for expert advice on what, as far as he is concerned, is essentially a cold case; and you cannot possibly travel in your present circumstances. We need to find an expert in UK!"

"My present circumstances! I finished a final round of chemotherapy last week and, as my oncologist is apparently unable to stop me from dying, I am certainly not going to let her stop me from living. Miss Wilson tells me she is not working at the moment, so she could accompany me to keep me out of trouble!"

Anya laughed gently. "Mr Chambers, one of the problems of being out of work is that I struggled to raise the bus fare to

149

come to Edinburgh, let alone find the money for a trip to Istanbul."

"And what makes you think you would have to pay for going to Istanbul? If you are to be my guardian, it will be my duty and pleasure to take you as my guest. As for John here, he is a wealthy man and can afford to buy his own plane ticket. No need to go bothering his superintendent. He must be due some leave."

Arbuthnot groaned. Niall had no idea of the complexity of what he was suggesting. While there was no problem about taking leave or funding the trip, he would have to discuss it with his superintendent and he would need to let Kadir Demercol know. The very thought of the difficult discussions ahead and the inevitable paperwork depressed him.

As gently as he could, Arbuthnot told Niall that he would need to think about the implications of a trip. Although, if he were being honest, the idea of going to Istanbul with Anya appealed to him. He and Anya would discuss the matter over dinner.

Chapter 16
Southend, December 1995

In a state of suspended belief, Anya found herself looking out her passport and packing for a trip to Istanbul. The prospect both alarmed and excited her. She felt drawn to John Arbuthnot, not with the intensity of the attraction to Amir, but there was something very warm and reassuring about him. At the same time, the thought of trusting anyone ever again frightened her.

He had certainly been very attentive to her in Edinburgh, but at no time had he given any indication that theirs was more than an entirely professional association. She was also anxious about travelling with Niall. She liked him immensely and admired his courage, but she knew nothing about caring for someone with terminal cancer, and the thought of anything going wrong in Istanbul and having to contact the British Consulate General for help filled her with panic.

She had had no contact with the Foreign and Commonwealth Office since that awful day in King Charles Street fourteen months ago, she knew her case had been the talk of the office in diplomatic posts around the world, and the prospect of having to face former colleagues in an emergency brought all the shame and humiliation of those frightening days flooding back.

She pulled herself together, nothing was going to go wrong and, scared or not, she was due at Gatwick airport at eight-thirty-five next morning.

As arranged, she went straight to the Special Assistance desk at the airport where John was waiting for her along with Niall beaming broadly from his wheelchair. The two men had travelled from Edinburgh the day before and had rested overnight at an airport hotel to break the journey.

"My wonderful companion has just arrived," Niall announced to the woman at the check in desk, and in a matter of minutes they had their boarding passes and were being swept through security and passport control, overtaking lines of weary travellers waiting in the endless queues which are the unavoidable reality of airline travel for those deemed fit enough to survive the experience.

The flight was uneventful and a helpful man from Special Assistance at Atatürk Airport ensured that visas were issued and a taxi hailed in record time.

Istanbul: Day 1

Standing outside the terminal building, Aydin Fenerbaçe stared tearfully at the departing Lufthansa 747 as it soared into the cloudless sky, taking his beloved Turkish daughter back to Germany where her husband had finally found work as a stonemason. Irony of a sort—for Aydin had been born Alfred Fischer and had spent his war years with the Einsatzstab Reichsleiter Rosenberg (ERR) assisting in the 'repatriation' of works of art from Holland and France to Germany.

By 1941, he had become indispensable to Ober Gruppen Führer Hans Peter von Seidel as together they removed selected items from consignments destined for the Fatherland. It had been a risky business, involving bribing guards at railway sidings where wagons loaded with paintings, statues and other valuables awaited departure under cover of darkness.

On the rare occasions when a guard refused to turn a blind eye to their activity, there had been no option but to silence him—permanently, increasing significantly the risk of discovery. All this, with the ever-present fear that Göring or, worse still, the Führer, would discover the extent to which Hans Peter and he were depriving the Third Reich of part of its new-found 'patrimony'.

He had been paid handsomely for his part in their joint endeavour but had never sought to retain any of the stolen works of art for himself. He had no contacts in the world where such things were bought and sold. Reichsmarks were all that had interested him and Hans Peter appeared to have an inexhaustible supply. While that supply lasted, Alfred Fischer's loyalty was assured. Fate then intervened.

By December 1942, Hans Peter had ceased to trust his Portuguese and Turkish carriers. Thus it was that, against his better judgement but persuaded by the recompense offered, Alfred had agreed to accompany the final consignment of paintings on its dangerous journey to Istanbul. The gruelling experience had taken five terrifying, exhausting and stressful months.

On the last leg of the journey, the captain of a Turkish fishing vessel had threatened to dump both Alfred and his cargo into the sea unless Alfred handed over every last

Reichsmark in his possession. Alfred had been left stranded and penniless in Istanbul, sleeping rough in different places every night to avoid police patrols and occasionally working illegally for a pittance at the docks or on building sites.

By the time the war ended, his carefully accumulated Reichsmarks in the Danziger Bank were worthless even if there had been the means to withdraw them, and he deeply regretted his decision to be paid in cash rather than in kind. Life as an illegal immigrant had not been easy, but he had been saved by catching the eye of the owner of a small and notably corrupt building firm.

The owner recognised intelligence and a kindred spirit when he saw it and before long, Alfred had proved invaluable in bribing, corrupting and intimidating the company's way to lucrative contracts. He was also the proud owner of a new identity, a set of very convincing counterfeit documents and the hand of the builder's daughter in marriage.

For the past fifty years, he had been Aydin Fenerbaçe, husband of Marissa, father of the beloved daughter who now lived in Germany and the son who ran the company Alfred had built up following his father-in-law's death. It had been transformed into a modestly successful business operating more or less within the law and generating sufficient income to support Alfred, Marissa and their son and his family.

It had not been enough to support his daughter and husband as well and they had left to seek their fortune in Germany—a country Alfred would never be able to visit as his wartime exploits were so closely linked to those of Hans Peter von Seidel, a much sought-after war criminal who had been declared missing presumed dead. Aydin knew better than that, of course.

Over the years, Hans Peter had bought Aydin's silence—to Aydin everything, including loyalty, had a price—and had asked him to keep an eye on any suspicious movements at the secure storage vault in Istanbul. It was Aydin who had alerted Hans Peter every time Albrecht came to the city and who had informed him that Albrecht had actually visited the vault soon after their father's death.

He had refused, however, to take part in the interrogation of Albrecht; he had considered it too risky and he had too much to lose if things went badly wrong. Hans Peter would have to come to Istanbul to arrange that for himself.

Following Albrecht's murder, he had kept Hans Peter abreast of local news coverage of the investigation, and eighteen months later, of the arrival of a British police officer suggesting that police had made the link between the murder of Albrecht and that of his friend in Scotland.

Unlike senior officers who seemed able to soar above war-time dangers, Aydin had been a private and he knew he would eventually have been sent from his comfortable billet to the Russian Front, or the Gothic Line or to the last desperate stand to save Berlin as the Russians advanced.

In the unlikely event that he survived any or several of these fates, he would have been hauled before a tribunal to answer for his part in the war time atrocities committed by his commanding officer, and for the large-scale theft of works of art. Therefore, however hard the journey by sea and across North Africa had been, or how tough the early years in Istanbul, he had Hans Peter to thank for the fact he had been sent on that mission and was still alive.

That said, the murder of Hans Albrecht had changed everything. It brought the past too close for comfort. From that moment onwards, he was determined that any help he gave von Seidel would be strictly limited to passing on information he could acquire at no risk to himself. He had done enough over the years to repay any debt he owed the man.

As the Lufthansa plane disappeared from view, Aydin turned sadly towards the car park, passing a line of tourists waiting impatiently for taxis to take them to their destination. He became aware of a slight frisson of annoyance ahead as an airport employee pushing a wheelchair cut in to the head of the queue depositing his charges in the first taxi in line.

As the taxi moved off, one of the passengers stared out of the window in his direction. It was the British policeman. Why was he back in Istanbul? Surely, it was just for a holiday. No policeman took a handicapped man and a woman with him on official business, did they? Unless it was as cover.

He had better find out. He ran to his car and eventually caught up with the taxi in the inevitable crush of traffic jostling between lanes on the main road into the city from the airport.

The taxi finally pulled up alongside a boutique hotel on a quiet side road not far from Topkapi Palace. The Hotel Sospiri was a traditional Istanbul town house, once home to a wealthy merchant who had fallen in love with Venice, hence the name. Beautiful period furniture and décor in the reception area and public rooms added to the timeless tranquillity of the place.

Niall was tired and elected to have a light refreshment sent to his room and to rest until dinner when they would be joined by Faisal Arslan. Arbuthnot took Anya to a cafe near the Museum of Islamic Art where he was welcomed back by the owner who remembered him from his earlier visit. No one paid much attention to a tall, elderly man who entered the café shortly afterwards.

There was just time to visit the magnificent Hagia Sofia before dinner. Built by the Byzantine Emperor Justinian in the sixth century over the ruins of two Constantinian churches, converted into a mosque in the fifteenth century, and deconsecrated following a major restoration in the twentieth century, it was now a museum.

Inside, Anya and John stared in wonder at the soaring dome, the magnificent pillars and the light streaming through windows high above the galleries. They admired the beautiful mosaic of the Virgin Mary dominating the apse, and the mosaics of emperors and saints decorating the walls of the galleries.

On the way back to the hotel, they stopped to admire the Blue Mosque, and Anya began to think about the sightseeing she and Niall might do by taxi the following day. She hoped she was up to the challenge of wheelchair tourism with a fascinating man whose boundless enthusiasm for the city was in inverse proportion to his depleted physical resources.

Dr Faisal Arslan breezed into the hotel dining room like a miniature tornado. He was small and round with a shock of grey hair which merged seamlessly into a dramatic beard. A magnificent high collared Turkish jacket floated behind him as he strode towards the table where the others were sitting and he broke into a huge smile as he set eyes on Niall.

"My dear friend, why have you been missing from Istanbul for so long? But...I see you have lost much weight! Are you unwell?"

"Nothing but a touch of old age," said Niall with a deprecating smile. "Now, sit down and let me make introductions. This wonderful lady is Angharad Wilson and she is the owner of the ring I have described to you; this rogue on my right is John Arbuthnot, a dear friend who spends his life investigating horrible crimes on behalf of the Scottish police—and that is what brings us here."

"Welcome to Istanbul!"

Anya and John instantly warmed to this man whose bright eyes and engaging smile enveloped their little group as he shook hands with each in turn.

Reaching for the menu, Faisal said, "Let's order before we do anything else. Perhaps some good Turkish food will put a little flesh back on these old bones of yours, Niall. Shall we start by sharing a large mezze—they make an excellent one here—then we can decide what we each want afterwards."

This suggestion was met with a murmur of assent and Faisal called over a waiter to interrogate him on exactly which roast vegetables, what kind of humous and yoghurt dips, what felafel, soft cheeses, breads and other delicacies would be included in this evening's offering.

Satisfied with the response, he ordered a mezze for four and asked the waiter to bring chilled water with a dash of lemon at once. The practicalities over, he took a magnifying glass from his pocket and asked Anya to show him the ring.

"Good Heavens, how utterly extraordinary! The first thing to say is that this inset did not start out life as part of a ring. Unfortunately, the back of the inset is partially hidden behind the gold mount, but I can see enough to hazard an educated guess."

"The inset almost certainly dates from the late seventeenth century and would have decorated the hilt of a ceremonial sabre, possibly a Janissary kilij. The workmanship is very fine indeed but if you look closely, you will see that there are fine marks on the raised surfaces. This tells me that at some point after being detached from the armament, it has been pressed into another surface like wax as a seal or as proof of identity."

Niall and he took turns staring through the magnifying glass at the inset and ring. "Another thing that puzzles me," said Niall, "is the engraving on the inside of the ring. It looks like the date of a marriage but has been engraved by someone with very little skill, unlike the goldsmith who re-modelled the ring in the first place."

"Why would someone who could afford an object like this perform what looks like a 'do-it-yourself' engraving to record an important event like a marriage."

Faisal turned the ring over. "I see what you mean. HLV19 11 00HPS, but I don't think it is the date of a marriage, I think it is a code of some sort. If the owner did not want anyone else to know this code, it could explain why he decided to engrave it himself. The tools aren't hard to come by, unlike having the necessary skill!"

"Do you think the insert and code could relate to a private bank account?" Arbuthnot asked.

Faisal laughed. "Even the Turkish banks have rather more sophisticated identity and security screening methods these days!"

"I wasn't thinking of normal banks, but perhaps one that operates below the radar. But you are right. It might have been the ring's original purpose many years ago, but I am sure even disreputable companies have introduced more effective identity procedures now."

"I think you should take it to the police and see what their experts make of it."

Arbuthnot was already a step ahead with an appointment scheduled with Chief Inspector Demercol at ten am next morning.

The rest of the evening was spent in convivial conversation. Niall had asked the hotel to arrange for a car and driver to be at their disposal the following day to take him and Anya on a tour past Hagia Sofia, the Blue Mosque, and finally to the architect Sinan's masterpiece, the Sülemaniye Mosque.

If his strength held out, he hoped also to visit the former Byzantine church of St Saviour in Chora to study the magnificent mosaics. John had said he couldn't join them in the morning, but Anya would be with him, and Niall looked forward to having her company all to himself.

Chapter 17
Istanbul, December 1995
Day 2

As he left next morning, Arbuthnot noticed a man reading a newspaper in a car parked opposite the hotel. It struck him as strange as parking was not allowed on the narrow street, but perhaps the man was just waiting for someone. As his taxi pulled away heading for police headquarters, Arbuthnot was sure he heard the other car start.

Was it fanciful or a policeman's instinct that made him wonder if the man had been watching him. He dismissed the idea as ridiculous. The car was a silver hatchback, but he had not registered the make, so many models looked alike these days and he regretted the lack of originality in design. Beautiful vintage cars were one of his private passions.

On the journey, he turned round several times to check and thought he saw a silver car two or three cars behind them, but five-door silver hatchbacks were ten a penny and he could not be sure it was the same car. John had Anya's ring in his pocket; the Turkish police were not inclined to allow foreign civilians to tag along in an investigation.

On arrival at police headquarters, Arbuthnot looked up and down the street but there was no sign of the silver car. *I must be becoming paranoid*, he thought. Entering the police headquarters, he double checked his inside pocket to ensure the ring was safe, then carefully removed it to place on a tray along with his keys and phone at security.

He had to restrain himself from leaning forward and grabbing the ring as soon as the tray emerged from screening, forcing himself to wait and collect it along with the rest of his belongings in what he hoped was an orderly fashion. The last thing he wanted to do was draw attention to it.

At the reception desk, a young woman confirmed that Chief Inspector Demercol was expecting him and would be along in a minute to escort him to his office. It was rare for the chief inspector to greet visitors in person and she treated Arbuthnot to the deference he clearly merited.

Demercol appeared, his face wreathed in smiles at the sight of his Scottish counterpart, and an unaccustomed glimmer of hope in his eyes. Had John Arbuthnot found the key to solving two high profile murders which had preoccupied them both, not to mention their superiors and political masters for almost four years?

Demercol had read Arbuthnot's report on the history and provenance of the ring, how and when the ring had resurfaced and Niall Chambers' evaluation of it; and Arbuthnot was able to fill him in on Professor Arslan's corroboration of Chambers' findings. Demercol studied the ring carefully then pulled a photograph from a file on his desk. It was a post-mortem photograph of Albrecht von Seidel.

"This ring may explain something which has puzzled us. If you look closely at the photograph, you will notice that von

Seidel's face, arms and hands were deeply tanned apart from a large circle at the base of the fourth finger of his right hand. The small ring he was wearing when we found him—I understand it was the kind of ring priests receive at ordination—in no way covered the untanned area on his finger."

"We figured he must have been wearing a much larger ring until shortly before his death. If that had been what his assailants were looking for, and had he been wearing it at the time, there would have been no need for the extreme brutality meted out to him. Furthermore, if his assailants had taken the ring by force, they would hardly have bothered to replace it with another one, nor would they have gone looking for Charles Gibson the following morning."

"It has always been our view, and yours too, that Albrecht von Seidel passed something to Charles Gibson for safe keeping just before he died. Could this ring be what we are looking for?"

Demercol made a quick call to a contact at the *Türkiye Bankalar Birliği* (Turkish Banks Association) and got the name of an expert in security for private bank customers and made an appointment to meet her later that morning. Azra Yilmaz turned out to be a striking woman in her mid-forties with piercing, intelligent eyes and an abrupt manner borne of many years working in a male dominated business.

"What an extraordinary thing," she said turning the ring over in her hands, a slight smile playing at the corners of her mouth. "I haven't seen anything like this outside of a museum, but it is certainly the sort of seal that would have been used in Ottoman times as proof of identity; and some smaller secure storage facilities may have used something similar as late as the mid twentieth century."

"By now, even they will have moved to electronic systems, key codes, or fingerprint recognition, etc. Unless, of course, a particular client cannot be traced, or has refused to accept the change."

As might be the case for a former war criminal declared missing presumed dead fifty years ago, Arbuthnot thought as he recalled Stefania von Seidel's and Hanna Brandt's conviction that Hans Peter was still alive.

Azra assured them there was no point in enquiring at Turkish banks where security for private customers had long since been computerised, but that it might be worth their while checking out older secure storage companies. The policemen thanked her for her time and her advice and wished her good day.

Outside her office, Demercol made a phone call to police headquarters asking for a list of secure storage facilities within a 4 kilometre radius of the Ariel Hotel where Albrecht von Seidel had been staying. Neither he nor John Arbuthnot noticed a silver hatchback pulling away on the far side of the street. Back at headquarters, they were presented with a depressingly long list of companies.

To begin with, Arbuthnot and Demercol were vaguely amused by the reactions of the owners of secure storage facilities when asked about how their private customers accessed their vaults. Responses ranged from business-like regret.

"We haven't used seals for identification since my great-grandfather's time,"; to genuine youthful puzzlement, "We set up business ten years ago; did people really use *seals* for identification in the old days?"; to blind panic at the sight of the ID cards and an over-robust denial that they had ever seen anything like the ring.

Demercol took a careful note of the companies in the last category for future reference. However, towards the end of the afternoon and with more than half the listed companies still to investigate, the humour of the situation had evaporated. Facilities were closing for the night and the tedious search would have to start again the next day.

Arbuthnot met Anya at their hotel for pre-dinner drinks and a round-up of the day's events, earlier hopes of a quick solution to the provenance and purpose of the ring fading fast. Arbuthnot had to leave the ring with the Turkish police in spite of his plea that Anya would be safer if it were in her possession. Niall joined them briefly and talked with almost childish excitement about all the places he had seen that day.

However, he was exhausted and opted for room service rather than a meal in the hotel restaurant. He wanted to be fit for his programme next day—a trip to a place his driver knew where he could have a spectacular view over the Bosphorus without being jostled by crowds, then on to lunch with his friend, Faisal Arslan.

As Niall was not dining with them, Anya and John Arbuthnot decided to try a local restaurant recommended by Kadir Demercol. As they left the hotel, John said, "There's that car again, parked further down the road this time."

"What car again?" Anya called to his retreating back as he walked purposely towards a silver-grey car which sped off, tires squealing in protest, before he reached it but not before Anya had noted the number plate.

"Well done! I'll get the police to trace the owner. However, if it is following me as I suspect, it is probably stolen."

Kadir Demercol called into the police station as his wife was serving dinner and asked a colleague to trace the ownership of the car, and, as an afterthought, asked him to send an officer to check the security cameras outside the offices of Azra Yilmaz and outside police headquarters.

By eleven pm, Demercol had been advised that the car was registered to an Aydin Fenerbaçe and that it had been parked outside the offices of Azra Yilmaz and police headquarters earlier that day at times which corresponded with his own itinerary.

Anya and Arbuthnot set off in search of the restaurant Kadir Demercol had recommended and found it in a steep, cobbled side street near the spice market. The restaurant had happily not succumbed to modernity in any of its garish manifestations—glass, chrome, tourist menus, loud music or echoing flooring. The dark, polished hard wood floor was covered with richly coloured Turkish rugs.

Floor-length damask table covers softened the starkness of white tablecloths, polished silver and crystal glasses. A smiling waiter immediately brought over a flask of chilled water and unfolded damask napkins with a practiced flourish. Their decision to follow the waiter's recommendations from a menu they would otherwise have struggled to navigate, and to accompany the exquisite dishes with a light, crisp rosé wine was amply rewarded.

At the end of a meal which had done much to compensate for the frustrations of the day, they walked back to the hotel. Worried by the thought that they were being followed,

Arbuthnot accompanied Anya to her second floor room, checked it out and showed her how to open the door quickly to give a wide view and flush out anyone hiding behind it.

As he bade her goodnight, he inadvertently brushed against her and for a moment, they held each other's gaze—sudden, powerful attraction battling with the wisdom of keeping the relationship on a strictly professional basis. Arbuthnot broke the spell, grasping Anya's hand in a theatrical gesture and giving it a chaste goodnight kiss. Both found sleep surprisingly elusive that night.

Chapter 18
Istanbul Airport
Day 2

Aydin Fenerbaçe, born Alfred Fischer, looked at his watch impatiently. It was almost midnight and he was kicking his heels outside International Arrivals at the airport following a blazing row with his wife. He was waiting for an impoverished Hans Peter von Seidel, due to arrive at any moment with no money for a taxi, lodging or anything else for that matter. His wife had flatly refused to have him in the house.

"That man is nothing but trouble. You owe him nothing. You say he saved your life, but that was half a century ago and by accident not design. Why does he still have such a hold over you?"

Aydin said nothing. There were many things his wife did not know about his war-time activities, and Hans Peter kept up the threat of exposing his past any time his willingness to help faltered. Thus it was that, much against his will, he had paid for two nights at a cheap hotel for Hans Peter, leaving an envelope in his room with just enough lire to keep him afloat for two days.

More than that he would not do, or so he vowed to himself for the umpteenth time. And in truth, he had been afraid for himself when he saw the British policeman at Istanbul airport the day before and even more afraid when he found out that he and the Turkish detective were going around storage facilities in the city centre.

If they tracked down Hans Peter's horde, it would take them no time to track down Alfred Fischer as well.

Bayan Fenerbaçe was not pleased to be woken at eleven fifteen pm by a phone call from the police asking if she was the owner of a silver Opal hatch back.

"My husband has an Opal hatch back. Why, has there been an accident?" She added, anxiety briefly over-riding annoyance.

"Not as far as we know, but have you any reason to think the car might have been stolen?"

"That's unlikely, unless my husband has managed to lose it since he left here an hour ago to drive to the airport!" She replied tartly still smarting from their earlier row.

"Why was he going to the airport?"

"Why do you want to know this?"

"Just answer the question, Bayan."

Bayan Fenerbaçe felt her legs giving way and she clutched onto the bedside table for support. This phone call frightened her. Hans Peter frightened her, and she had always been worried by the hold he exerted over her husband. Hans Peter's sudden appearance spelled danger and she didn't understand what this was about. All she knew was that Aydin had been lying to her recently and she didn't know why.

"He is meeting a business client. No, I'm sorry, I don't know his name," she stammered.

"Am I expected to believe that you do not know who your husband has gone to meet at this time of night?"

"You can believe whatever you like, but I can't tell you what I don't know. You will need to ask him."

"Believe me, we shall. Please ask your husband to contact us when he gets home if he knows what is best for him."

Bayan Fenerbaçe dropped the receiver onto the cradle as if it were red hot. Her hands were shaking. She would wait up till Aydin returned. It was time for some straight talking.

Mogadishu: December 1995: Earlier That Day

The former colonial villa in which Hans Peter von Seidel now lived could not have been more different from his childhood home in Bavaria, or his estate in Argentina. Paint and plaster flaked off the stained exterior walls, dirty windows sheltered behind the scant protection of ancient, rusted bars, and a once-elegant front door showed the signs of many uninvited intrusions since Mogadishu had descended into chaos following the fall of its dictator, Said Barre.

The interior was dark and smelled musty. The tattered furnishings left in haste by a departing Italian diplomat decades before, had long since lost any pretence at comfort or elegance. The erratic power supply did little to pierce the gloom and his telephone—when it worked—was almost certainly tapped. A once carefully tended Italianate garden was now a tangled mass of scrub and litter, the outline of its geometric paths and borders barely visible amid the disarray.

The loyal German bodyguards who had served him well for the first twenty years of his exile had been replaced by increasingly unreliable local thugs, including the two he had

170

been forced to relieve of their duties and their lives near Izmir three years previously. For the first time since his flight from Germany fifty years earlier, Hans Peter von Seidel felt scared and at a loss to know how to resolve his difficulties.

He was deeply in debt to men who took a very dim view of unpaid bills, not just in Mogadishu but in Scotland where the notorious Manson brothers waited in mounting impatience for final payment for the services of the two heavies sent on his behalf to visit Dr Gibson. They knew where he lived and they had threatened to send 'representatives' to collect on their behalf.

Wanted for war crimes in Europe, Israel and Argentina, his Dutch cover identity blown and absolutely broke, he had run out of places to hide. It was a ridiculous situation all things considered. Works of art worth millions of dollars lay in a secure vault in Istanbul, protected by an elaborate security system he himself had installed during the 1930s.

He knew the security code, but without the ring, the vault might as well have been on the moon. On the eve of his flight from Germany in 1945, he had entrusted the ring to his father who had lost no time in asserting his belief in Hans Peter's death when it looked as if the MFAA were moving in on the family art dealing business.

And his father had finally given the ring to Albrecht of all people! Albrecht who, had he lived, would have spent every last pfennig of the von Seidel fortune ensuring that the contents of the vault were returned to their so-called 'rightful' owners! He could not have allowed that to happen, not after the years of effort and anxiety accumulating the collection and arranging for its complicated and costly dispatch to Turkey.

171

When his men failed to find the ring in Albrecht's hotel room, he had been convinced that Albrecht had passed it to Charles Gibson. However, that search too had ended in a violent death and no ring. Sadly, the present day criminal classes lacked the sophisticated interrogation techniques of the SS—techniques which had ensured that a prisoner remained alive until he or she had divulged whatever information was sought.

If, as in all probability, Albrecht or Charles had left the ring to Hans Dietrich's daughter, Magdalena, he had no means of extracting it, or of paying others to do so, on his behalf. That scourge Wiesenthal had managed to convince the German authorities that he was probably still alive and his current, low budget documentation would not stand up to Germany's sophisticated border controls.

Germany was not a country he could enter without finding himself under clamorous arrest, he had no contacts in the German underworld and no means to pay them even if he had.

His fevered mind played endlessly over how to get into the Istanbul vault. Just one or two of the smaller paintings—a Matisse and a Degas perhaps—could solve his present financial difficulties. There was no point in threatening the current owner of the secure storage facility. The new owner did not have access to the vault—a safeguard he had personally built into the system.

The new owner was also a very different man from his morally fluid grandfather with whom Hans Peter had conducted his original dealings in the 1930s. On a recent, high risk attempt to gain access to the vault without the identity ring, the tight-lipped young owner had queried Hans Peter's credentials as his records showed that Hans Peter von Seidel was deceased as were his father and brother.

As the owner had no new instruction as to ownership of, or access to the vault, he had advised Hans Peter to leave at once if he did not want the police called. Hans Peter had the uneasy feeling that the police would be called in any case, just as soon as he left. The last thing he needed was to come to the attention of the Turkish police.

The phone rang jolting him out of feverish attempts to find a solution to his seemingly intractable problems. The voice on the other end of the line belonged to another fugitive from war-time Germany who had been hiding under a false identity in the sprawling outskirts of Istanbul for the best part of fifty years.

"I thought you should know that the British policeman is back in Istanbul. He was seen visiting storage facilities with Chief Inspector Demercol this afternoon." The line went dead and long-suppressed fears rose in a confusion of nightmarish images destroying all capacity for rational thought.

He picked up the last of his dollars and his false Swedish passport and headed for the airport. Despite the intense heat, a cold sweat broke out over his body and an overwhelming panic gripped him. He struggled unsuccessfully to still the turmoil in his mind and work out what the police were doing in Istanbul.

They must have new information if the British policeman had arrived. Had Albrecht visited the vault and told someone what he had found? No, if he had done so the police would have found the vault long ago. And his contact had said the police were visiting storage facilities, not just one facility, so they could not know everything.

Had the police found the ring? Had all his efforts been in vain? He felt sick with apprehension.

His mind went back to the early years of the war when all of Europe seemed within Germany's grasp. As Alfred Rosenberg's right-hand man in the Einsatzstab Reichsleiter Rosenberg (ERR), he had worked tirelessly to trace works of art coveted by the German High Command, before 'liberating' them from their mainly Jewish owners.

When that source began to dry up as a result of other policies of the German High Command, he had turned his attention towards museums in occupied France and the Netherlands. It had not taken him long to discover that Rosenberg was more interested in quantity than in quality, and by the early 1940s, he had begun the risky process of holding back a few high value items from each raid.

It was a costly business, first buying the silence of the few soldiers who knew what he was doing, then paying for secret shipments via Portugal and onwards to Istanbul. As the war drew on, the costs rose dramatically until even he could no longer afford the sum demanded by the increasingly nervous master of the fishing vessel used for the final stage of the perilous journey across the Mediterranean.

No matter. By then, he had a vast fortune safely stored in a vault in Istanbul. *His future was secure,* or so he had thought.

At eleven pm that night, he joined a long queue of incoming passengers at Istanbul airport as they made frustratingly slow progress towards the desk where a bored official would check passport details before issuing a tourist visa. Passport checks alarmed him more than ever now that he could no longer afford the services of skilled forgers. He

174

hoped Alfred Fischer would be waiting outside for him with comforting news.

Alfred did not immediately recognise the stooped, haggard-looking man who finally exited the terminal building at midnight. Hardship had taken its toll and Hans Peter's barely controlled nervous tension seemed to infuse the car as they made their way towards the city centre.

He made no secret of his dismay that Alfred could tell him nothing about why the British policeman had arrived, or who his companions were, or why police had resumed an active interest in Albrecht's murder, or what had prompted them to visit storage facilities.

All that Alfred could tell him was where the British party were staying, that Commander Demercol was leading the investigation, and that so far they had not visited the storage facility in Yasmak Siyiran Sok.

Alfred stopped the car outside a cheap hotel. It took some time to rouse a disgruntled night porter to let them in. Alfred helped Hans Peter to register as Per Svensson, newly arrived from Sweden and with passport to match.

As he prepared to take his leave, insisting he could do no more for his former superior officer, Hans Peter grabbed him roughly by the arm. His glare had lost none of its former ferocity and his words, quietly spoken, were full of menace.

"I need someone to drive me around the city tomorrow, and you need to remember just how difficult I could make things for you. So, be here at nine am if you value your comfortable lifestyle and happy family...AYYYDINN, or whatever you call yourself now!"

Alfred was on the verge of tears as he started the car. Would he never be rid of von Seidel and his infinite capacity to threaten everything he held dear. He was terrified at the prospect of the day ahead, of being arrested, of being found unjustly complicit in a murder and justly complicit in war-time atrocities and art theft on a grand scale.

Whatever Hans Peter had in mind for the day, it would not stop at a simple tour of the city by car. That much he knew.

As he approached his villa, he saw the unmarked vehicle parked under the trees on the opposite side of the road. Some sixth sense warned him that it was waiting for him and he made the decision that would drastically alter the course of his life. He made an abrupt U-turn, wheels screaming as they clipped the verge and accelerated away at high speed.

In his rear mirror, he saw the unmarked car make the same manoeuvre, the distance between them shortening alarmingly. He had the advantage of familiarity with the area and for a while hoped he had lost his pursuers in the maze of narrow roads and alleyways around his home, until he found his way blocked by a refuse lorry on a leisurely early morning round. Behind him the headlights of a powerful car rounded the corner flooding the narrow lane with unwelcome light.

He was trapped. He jumped out of his car, squeezed past the refuse lorry and its surprised driver and ran for his life, but years of good living had taken a toll on his fitness and in a short time, he was struggling for breath. Doubled up with a debilitating stitch in his side, he heard the footsteps closing in on him.

At nine-twenty am, Hans Peter called Alfred's home number to be greeted by his hysterical wife.

"Why have you come here? What have you done to Aydin? Why do you bring nothing but trouble for us?"

"Where is Aydin?"

"Where is Aydin!" She screamed. "The police were waiting for him when he got home last night and he has been arrested. No one will tell me why and I am not allowed to see him. They have taken all his personal documents, our car has been impounded and I have been told not to leave home as a detective is coming to question me!"

The phone went dead. Hans Peter checked out of his room just before ten am and left on foot, heading for the Hotel Sospiri, a boutique hotel in the old town. It would take him almost two hours to get there but it was the only thing he could think of doing. The small amount of money Alfred had left for him would barely cover the cost of a taxi to the airport and he knew he might need that if he had to escape in a hurry.

He hoped the woman or the invalid would be at the Hotel Sospiri and could be persuaded to tell him what the police knew and what they were looking for. He would need to act quickly—he had no doubt Alfred would eventually offer to tell the whole story in exchange for lenient treatment.

At eight am, Aydin Fenerbaçe, otherwise known as Alfred Fischer, sat at a metal table in an interview room at police headquarters. Facing him on the other side of the table were Chief Inspector Kadir Demercol of the Istanbul Serious Crime Unit, and Chief Inspector John Arbuthnot of Lothian and Borders Police, Scotland.

A translator sat on a chair to one side and a uniformed police officer stood guard at the door. The door opened briefly as a bored looking duty lawyer was ushered in.

It took very little time to dismantle Aydin Fenerbaçe's hastily concocted account of his activities over the last twenty-four hours. According to him, a Swedish business contact had called him asking if he would keep tabs on an

Englishman who had defrauded him and who, he believed, was in Istanbul. This would only be until his contact, Per Svensson, was able to get to Istanbul to take over the matter himself.

As Aydin's business was experiencing some cash flow problems and as the remuneration offered for following the Englishman was good, it seemed too good an opportunity to miss. As he had told the arresting officers, Mr Svensson arrived late the previous evening and he had driven him to his hotel.

When he was almost at home, he realised there was something he should have told Mr Svensson, and turned round to go back to the hotel, at which point he realised he was being chased by an unmarked car. Fearing a hijack, he had tried unsuccessfully to shake off his pursuers not knowing they were police.

The door of the interview room opened and a policewoman handed a file to Demercol who showed it to Arbuthnot.

"Mr Fenerbaçe, how did you get to know Mr Svensson in the first place?"

"We met on a construction site in Sweden just before the war."

"Where exactly in Sweden?"

It was at a time like this that Alfred Fischer wished fervently that he had paid more attention to geography lessons at school.

"Oslo," he replied.

"How odd. Oslo was in Norway last time I checked," observed Demercol with a wry smile.

"Norway/Sweden, what's the difference?…It was a long time ago," Fischer stammered.

"Quite a significant difference to those who live there, I believe," replied Demercol.

"Mr Fenerbaçe, while you were resting in one of our cells overnight, two of my colleagues visited Mr Svensson's hotel and a helpful night porter gave them a photocopy of Mr Svensson's passport. I have just received confirmation from the Swedish Consulate General that this passport is false. They have no record of a Per Svensson matching any of the details given on that document."

"The thing is, Mr Fenerbaçe, we have reason to believe that your friend, Per Svensson, is actually a wanted war criminal, Hans Peter von Seidel, brother of Monsignor Hans Albrecht von Seidel who, you may recall from the extensive media coverage at the time, was murdered in an Istanbul hotel four years ago."

"We have reason to believe that Hans Peter von Seidel was complicit in the murder of his brother and also in the murder of a Scottish academic in Edinburgh the following year, hence the presence of my Scottish colleague at this interview. I am not sure how severe the sentences are for aiding and abetting a war criminal and suspected murderer, but you can see where our questioning is leading…"

Aydin saw all too clearly. He heard his own voice shouting a desperate prolonged, "NO-O-O! I had nothing to do with any murders!" As the room seemed to swirl around him causing him to grab the edge of the table to steady himself.

"There is another thing that puzzles us, Mr Fenerbaçe. We have studied the documents your wife kindly retrieved for us and we can't find any trace of you since the date of your birth until your marriage in 1947—no high school certificates, no photographs, no record at all of your childhood. Well, things get lost of course, so perhaps you can fill in the detail for us. Where did you go to school, Mr Fenerbaçe?"

"G-go to school? What has that got to do with anything, I am seventy-five!"

"Just answer the question!"

In panic, Alfred gave the name of the school his son had attended, almost immediately cursing his own stupidity. He had worked on the construction site for that school in 1950, he could not possibly have attended it. Did Demercol know how old the school was? It hardly mattered. He would find out soon enough.

"Two things struck us as odd when we checked your papers against official records. There is no record of a passport being issued to you until 1956—nothing particularly surprising about that, people didn't travel much in those days, but you said you met your friend, Per Svensson, on a Swedish construction site before the war."

"How was that possible if you didn't have a Turkish passport? Did you enter Sweden illegally, or by using a passport in a different name, or were you never in Sweden at all?"

Alfred made no response, staring fixedly at a mark on one of his shoes.

"I mentioned another thing that puzzles us. We have found the record of a child named Aydin Fenerbaçe, born on the same day as the date-of-birth given in your papers, but we also found his death certificate showing that he died of influenza three months later."

"The best thing you can do for yourself, Mr Fenerbaçe, is to tell us who you really are; how you came to be involved with Hans Peter von Seidel; how, when and why you came to Turkey and assumed a Turkish identity; why you have maintained contact with von Seidel over the years when everyone else thought he was dead; and what exactly von Seidel is doing in Istanbul at this very moment. Take all the time you need."

As Alfred continued to stare disconsolately at his shoe, he knew that it was all over—fifty years of hard work, a happy marriage, adored children and grandchildren, good friends and a comfortable future, all wrecked in the space of twenty-four hours by one evil man. White anger consumed him and he decided to tell, to tell everything he knew about von Seidel. He would take the bastard down with him.

"My original name was Alfred Fischer..." he began, stopping as the door opened again and Demercol signalled for him to stop. A policewoman handed Demercol a note and he swore under his breath. The note stated that von Seidel had given the plain clothes officer following him the slip near the spice market.

"Before you start with your life story, tell us where von Seidel is going this morning! Quickly now, man!"

Alarmed by the sudden change of tack, Alfred stammered that he didn't know.

"Von Seidel wanted me to drive him around the city today so that he could find out why the police were suddenly interested in his brother's murder again, and why they were visiting storage facilities. He said something about maybe getting the woman or the invalid to talk."

Arbuthnot was already out of his seat.

"How would he know where to find them?" He barked in English barely concealing his frustration as he waited for the interpreter to translate his question and the response.

"He knows where they are staying. I told him last night!"

"I need to go," said Arbuthnot as he headed for the door.

"I'll follow with back up just as soon as I am sure this man is safely locked up. His life story can wait. Incidentally Fischer, which storage facility did von Seidel use?"

"I think it is in Yasmak Siyiran Sok."

Further out than the places we have visited so far, Demercol thought, quickly issuing orders for unmarked cars and armed police to go to the hotel—no sirens; and for covert coverage along Yasmak Siyiran Sok.

A plain clothes police woman was waiting for Arbuthnot at the front entrance and they ran across the courtyard to an unmarked car. It was already mid-day. The police woman drove at break-neck speed across the city, dodging trams and leaving a trail of blaring horns and shaking fists in her wake.

Arbuthnot would have been scared out of his wits had the urgency of getting to the hotel and protecting Anya and Niall not been foremost in his mind. They would probably be back at the hotel by now. Niall had been tired this morning and all they had planned to do was drive to Dolmahbaçe Palace to look out over the Bosphorus then return for lunch.

Arbuthnot pulled himself together, professionalism overcoming fear. He needed to make some quick calculations. How long was it since Demercol had got the message about von Seidel giving police the slip—not more than twenty minutes, add five to ten minutes for the phone call to be made and the message to reach the interview room.

Von Seidel had been at the spice market half an hour ago, and the spice market was no more than twenty minutes on foot from their hotel. Fear reasserted its grip. He leapt out of the car as soon as it drew up at the hotel entrance, telling the police woman to keep an eye on the exit until Demercol's men arrived, but on no account to confront anyone leaving. Just watch where they went.

The receptionist confirmed that Anya and Niall Chambers had returned just before mid-day and had gone up to their rooms. Mr Chambers had come down again shortly afterwards and had gone out with the friend who had dined with them the first evening. Miss Wilson was still in her room.

"Did anyone ask for her at the desk or by phone?"

"Yes, a gentleman came in and asked for Miss Wilson's room number. I didn't give it to him of course and he told me to call her and say that John wanted to see her urgently and that he had forgotten her room number. I asked if I could give him the number and she said yes."

"I need a pass key, now! That man is not called John. I am and Miss Wilson may be in danger."

"I'll come with you. I can't give pass keys out."

They took the stairs two at a time.

Chapter 19

It was only as she put the receiver down that it occurred to Anya that there was something odd about the phone call from reception. John had been to her room two or three times and even if he had forgotten the number, he knew exactly where it was. She felt vaguely uneasy. The bedroom door didn't have a spy hole, but it had a security chain. She would be able to check that it was John before opening the door fully.

As he took the lift to the second floor, Hans Peter congratulated himself on how easy it had been to fool the receptionist and Miss Wilson. It had been clever of Alfred to follow her into the hotel yesterday afternoon and listen as she gave her name and collected her room key.

Unfortunately, the key had been handed over without mention of the room number, but he had got round that small problem surprisingly easily. John Arbuthnot's identity he already knew from following media coverage of the unsuccessful police investigation into Charles Gibson's murder. The photograph Alfred had taken outside a storage facility the day before showed Demercol and Arbuthnot returning to their car.

There was no doubt. It was the same man. Getting arrested had been much less clever on Alfred's part, but Hans Peter reassured himself it could have nothing to do with him. All Alfred had done for him was to drive around town for a day and pick up a Swedish man from the airport. Nothing illegal in that; the arrest was probably just for a traffic offence or for some questionable business deal.

Still, he regretted not having Alfred with him for the task ahead. It had been a long time since he had carried out an interrogation and he was not as fit as he had been in those days.

He stood to the side of the door as he knocked so that she would have to open it wide to check who it was. He heard a chain sliding across and a hesitant voice asking, "Is that you, John?"

"Yes," he whispered. The door opened on the chain and he barged into it with his shoulder, pain numbing his arm as the chain was ripped from the wooden door frame. The woman screamed as she fell backwards onto the floor. He was on top of her in seconds pinning her arms to her sides. She screamed again and he struck her hard across her face.

"Do that again, and I'll kill you!" He hissed, spittle landing on her cheek. He forced her over onto her front, his knee pressed into the small of her back, immobilising her, while he tied her wrists behind her back. As he got to his feet, he was pleased to note that his old skills had not abandoned him.

"I have a knife," he said, pressing the point into the side of her neck lest she be in any doubt. "Get up and walk over to that chair. Now sit!" Anya cried out in pain as she felt her arms being yanked upwards and over the back of the chair.

"Any more noise and I'll kill you. Your life is nothing to me."

She kicked out wildly as he tried to tie her ankles and was rewarded with a deep knife slash down her left calf. The fight went out of her and she watched helplessly as he tied her ankles to the legs of the chair while a pool of bright red blood spread out across the floor. He crossed the room and quietly closed and locked the door. She watched in terror as he made a tourniquet from a section of the cord for closing the curtains.

"Do what I tell you or I will cut this and let you bleed out, though I might have some fun with you first."

Anya's legs were trembling and to her horror, she felt a trickle of warm urine run along her thighs.

"Now tell me where the ring is and this can be over quickly."

"I don't have it, you can look for yourself."

"Oh I shall," he said leaning over her menacingly. "Starting from here!" In one swift movement, his knife sliced open her blouse and he ripped the gold chain from her neck tossing it onto the floor. She felt the point of the knife against her breast as he said, "Let's start again, shall we. Where is the ring?"

"The Turkish police have it."

This time he hit her so hard that she and the chair fell over onto the floor. "Stupid bitch," he hissed. "Do you expect me to believe that you would simply hand over a ring that could open the door to a fortune?"

"It's true," she mumbled through an aching jaw, the metallic taste of blood in her mouth.

He righted the chair roughly. "Let's see if this improves your memory," he said, clasping one hand over her broken mouth and with the other slitting her bra and twisting her

186

nipple letting the knife fall to her lap. The pain was excruciating, her scream muffled by his hand.

"The truth this time, otherwise the pain is going to get very much worse and the damage will be permanent." He let go of her breast and picked up the knife again, circling her nipple with the blade.

"The ring isn't here, we gave it to the Turkish police, I…" She felt her eye socket crack as his fist rammed into her left eye. The chair rocked backwards but righted itself again.

Standing outside the door, John Arbuthnot heard the rough tones of a man's voice and the sound of movement. Did he imagine it, or did he hear a muffled groan?

"I need to see what's happening in there," he whispered to the anxious receptionist.

"Shall I open the door?" The young man asked.

"No, we don't know what is happening inside and we could make things much worse by charging in. Do all the rooms on this floor have balconies?"

"Yes, but there is quite a gap between the balconies if you're thinking of reaching Miss Wilson's from another room."

"That is exactly what I am thinking of doing. Quick, let me into the next room."

"I don't know if it's occupied," said the young man.

"I don't care if the president is in there with his mistress, open that door!"

Once out onto the balcony, John Arbuthnot saw that the young man had not been exaggerating about the distance between one balcony and the next, nor was he sure how secure the ornate wrought iron railings were. There was nothing for it but to trust to fate. He climbed gingerly over the railings being careful not to look down, grabbing the posts with both hands and letting his body fall, then edging slowly to the side.

Cautiously, he released one hand and reached for the nearest railing post on Anya's balcony, grabbing hold just as the sinews on his other arm reached screaming point. With a final heave, he swung his body towards Anya's balcony taking his full weight on one arm again for an agonising second as he released his hold on the first set of railings and grabbed for the second.

Pulling his dead weight up and over the balcony railings almost defeated him but with one final adrenaline-fuelled effort, he swung his feet onto the wall to gain some traction, pulled his knees and finally his feet onto the outer edge and clambered over onto the balcony of Anya's room.

Soundlessly, he peered through a gap in the curtains and what he saw chilled him to the bone. There was no time to contact Kadir Demercol or to make plans. Thankful that this was a listed building with secondary glazing rather than double glazing, he broke the glass beside the window catch, leant in, opened the French window and slid the secondary glazing back.

Hans Peter spun round at the sound of breaking glass and as John clambered awkwardly into the room, he pulled a gun—Alfred's gun—from his waist band and pointed it at John. He had hoped to avoid using the gun; guns made too much noise and left too much evidence behind, but John Arbuthnot was too large and too fit for close combat with a knife.

As he prepared to fire, Anya tipped her chair over striking Hans Peter as she and the chair fell and the bullet embedded itself harmlessly in the wall. John lunged at Hans Peter and the gun went off again. This time the bullet grazed John's shoulder.

Hans Peter fired again, but this time there was only a dry click as John rugby tackled his assailant. Still tied to the chair and lying on her side, Anya could barely see what was happening. Unable to move her arms or legs to break her fall, she had taken the full weight of it on her left side. Blood from a head wound mixed with tears blurred her already compromised vision.

Hans Peter had grabbed the knife as he staggered back under John's gathering momentum, landing heavily and awkwardly on his back. After a desperate struggle, John managed to land a hard blow just under Hans Peter's rib cage leaving him fighting for breath. The knife fell and John grabbed it, knowing that he needed to end this quickly.

He was losing blood from his shoulder wound and the pain was crippling. The adrenaline was draining from his system and he felt himself weakening as he steeled himself to use the knife. Without warning, the bedroom door shattered before his eyes and four heavily armed police burst into the room.

In a final act of defiance, Hans Peter turned the gun on himself but was rewarded with nothing but another dry click. Alfred had not been in the habit of keeping his gun fully loaded. It was all over so quickly. Hans Peter was overpowered and led manacled from the room to face a future behind bars in whichever country finally won the contest to be first to bring him to trial and sentence him.

Paramedics arrived to stabilise Anya and John before taking them off to hospital. Kadir Demercol accompanied John in the ambulance.

"I am trying to work out which of the many breaches of Turkish law and international police protocol I should charge you with," he said, the ghost of a smile crossing his face. "And perhaps I should add assault, violent affray and damage to hotel property as well!"

"Might as well just throw the book at me," John replied, grimacing as the ambulance swung round a corner sending shafts of pain searing through his chest and shoulder. "What took you so long to turn up, anyway?"

"Oh, I stopped for a coffee and a manicure on the way! I didn't think you'd mind. It was fascinating watching your antics on the balconies though, but I think you should stick with the day job rather than joining the circus!"

As the ambulance pulled up at the entrance to Göztepe Hospital, Kadir announced airily that he was about to leave John to his fate at the hands of Istanbul's finest surgeons. He, on the other hand, would head off towards his own uncertain fate at an urgent meeting called by his superintendent.

His hope was that the kudos of arresting the murderer of a prominent German art historian, two as yet unidentified African hit men and a Scottish academic—not to mention the discovery of a vast horde of looted paintings and sculpture—would convince his superintendent to overlook the raft of breaches of protocol and procedure that had led to these successes!

A press conference was scheduled at police headquarters for late afternoon and, predictably, Kadir's director and superintendent basked in triumph as they announced these major developments to a frenzied international press corps, making little more than passing reference to the contribution of a Scottish policeman and of their own, aristocratic chief inspector to one of Istanbul police force's finest hours.

Kadir arranged to visit John later in the day to tell him what his colleagues had found in a vast vault in Yasmin Siyrian Sok. It promised to be an astounding revelation! In the meantime, he had placed armed guards at the hospital in case von Seidel had any other friends hovering in the vicinity.

Chapter 20
Göztepe Hospital,
Two Days Later

Anya felt as though she were clambering up through a steep, dark tunnel towards a pinpoint of light. Her head felt as if it were in a vice and for some reason she couldn't move her left leg. With a stifled gasp, she finally emerged into a blaze of white light.

Where was she? She seemed to be pinned down on a bed. Was she a prisoner? Prisoners were often subjected to constant bright light, weren't they? Terrifying images of a scarred man emerged then receded as a wall of pain forced all other thought from her mind. Why could she not move? Was the man with the knife here?

There had been the sound of shattering glass and a shot. Her chair crashing to the floor—searing pain. John, dear God, was John dead? A surprisingly gentle voice broke into her feverish attempts to make sense of what was happening around her, saying something soothing in words she didn't understand.

She tried to turn her head in the direction of the sound causing an explosion of pain to shoot from her lower jaw to her forehead, and down her left side to her ankle. More gentle words were accompanied by light fingertips on her shoulders urging her back onto her pillow.

"Good, you awake, Miss Wilson, but plis not move. Move not good."

The blurred face of a young woman appeared through the haze of light, but there seemed to be something wrong with her field of vision. In rising panic, she realised she was unable to see out of her left eye. Gingerly, she raised a hand towards her eye and encountered bandages. She felt her hand being moved gently back to her side.

"Have I lost the sight in my eye?" She tried to ask, gasping at the painful effort involved in trying to open her mouth.

"No, doctor come one minute and speak."

True to her word, a door opened and an attractive middle-aged woman walked in, a broad smile on her face. Her hair was caught up in a turban-style headscarf and the rest of her was covered in green surgical scrubs.

"I'm glad to find you awake, Miss Wilson. You have given us rather a lot of work since your arrival two days ago. I am the surgeon who operated on your jaw and eye socket. I have had to put a pin in your jaw unfortunately, but you should make a good recovery from both injuries with very little scarring."

"I don't think there is any damage to your eye, but I shall ask a specialist to look at it tomorrow, just to be sure. The surgeon who fixed your leg will be along later. He tells me that you may require further surgery but that you should get full functionality back in time."

"Thank you," Anya mumbled through serried lips. "but where am I?"

"Göztepe Hospital. You were brought in two days ago by the police. It seems you were the victim of a very violent attack. I am sorry I don't know any more than that. We have kept you in an induced coma for forty-eight hours to help you to recover with as little post-operative pain as possible."

If what she was experiencing now was minimised pain, Anya dreaded to think what awaited her when the drugs wore off. She had lost two days; slowly the frightening images of what took place in her hotel room began to take shape...

Anya grabbed the doctor's arm, mindless of the discomfort. "John! John Arbuthnot—do you know where the Scottish policeman is? Is he alright?"

"Shh. It is best if you try not to talk. I believe he is doing well and has been pleading endlessly with anyone who will listen to be allowed to visit you."

"Can he come now, please?"

"I think it would be better if we gave you something to help you sleep first, then we can let him visit when you wake up."

"I have already slept for two days, I don't need to sleep now, please can I see him."

"Very well, but only for ten minutes. I am going to leave you for a while, but the nurse will stay with you. I'll be back this evening to check that all is well."

Shortly afterwards, Anya heard the rumble of wheels in the corridor outside her room and a comfortingly familiar voice remonstrating with someone.

"I am not rolling into Miss Wilson's room in a wheelchair! I am perfectly able to walk, thank you!"

Whispered objections dispersed unheeded as John entered the room unsteadily, an anxious male nurse close behind him.

194

Anya almost laughed before remembering that laughing would invoke the torments of hell.

It was a rather different John from the smart, well-dressed man she was used to seeing. He was wearing pyjama trousers and one arm and shoulder were tightly strapped to a bare torso. His face was alight with remorse and concern.

"Anya, I am sorry. I am so, so sorry. I should never have allowed you to come to Istanbul with me or left you alone."

"John, there is no need to feel bad about this. I volunteered, with enthusiasm, if I remember rightly. But next time you decide enter my room, why not try the door rather than the window."

John sat on the chair beside her and held her hand, the gesture infinitely comforting and, at the same time, strangely exciting. After a moment, Anya started as a thought suddenly crossed her mind, "Niall; what has happened to Niall if we have been here for two days?"

"He is alright. He is staying with Faisal Arslan. Fortunately, by the time they rolled back from lunch, the immediate crisis was over, but they found the hotel bristling with police and forensic experts. Faisal took charge of the situation, sent a policeman to Niall's room to collect his belongings and took him home with him."

"Niall has been phoning the hospital several times a day, every day to find out how you are. He is not in the least concerned about me whom he rightly blames for everything that has happened to you!"

"Whew, I am glad he is safe."

"Von Seidel is currently the unhappy guest of the Turkish police who are asking him, none too politely I gather, about the death of Albrecht von Seidel and of two men found in a car near Izmir shortly afterwards. He is also being questioned about the attempted murder of you, and about the hundreds, literally hundreds of stolen art works found in a rented vault in Yasmin Siyrian Sok."

"The world press has gone mad and versions of the story—some even approximating to the truth—are on the front covers of the international press and on the main news channels world-wide. Meanwhile, Istanbul is heaving with officials from Interpol, representatives of French, Dutch, Belgian and Italian museums and galleries, individual claimants and representatives of every agency known to have an interest in artwork stolen during the war."

"The Ministry in Ankara is dealing with calls from Ministers of Culture from all over Europe; and the Wiesenthal Institute, British, Israeli, Dutch, French and Italian Governments want him brought to trial for war crimes."

"At some point, I hope to be able to ask von Seidel about the death of Charles Gibson but, at the moment, the queue of important people wanting to interview him is rather long and the Turkish police have made it clear that they want to deal with crimes committed in Turkey first."

"As far as Lothian and Borders police are concerned, I think we can safely say we know who orchestrated Charles Gibson's death. Unfortunately, we will probably never find out who actually carried out the murder. The information from Alfred Fischer—the man who was tailing us—is that von Seidel hired hit men from a Glasgow gangland boss he met in Tangier to interrogate Dr Gibson."

"Fischer alleges they were meant to threaten Gibson, rough him up a little if he didn't cooperate, but to stop short of killing him. Apparently, two erstwhile Mogadishan hit men, now regrettably deceased, were not supposed to kill Albrecht von Seidel either. It would appear that Hans Peter has been singularly unsuccessful in getting his hirelings to stick to their brief."

"Meanwhile, my superintendent will call on Glasgow gangland's finest at the Manson's elegant mansion in leafy Bearsden—an upmarket suburb to the north of the city. It's not difficult to imagine how the meeting will go. A sharp-suited flunky will usher the super through rooms where the eye-watering cost of the furnishings will be in inverse proportion to aesthetic taste—the itinerary selected to impress the policeman with Manson's ostentatious wealth and elevated status."

"The super will eventually find himself in a large study, walls lined with unread, leather-bound books and trophies from exclusive golf clubs. He will be offered—and will have to decline, one of the fine whiskies displayed along the up-lit shelves of a glittering glass and chrome bar. Manson will welcome him as a long-lost friend, his proffered hand revealing a jewel-encrusted Rolex and an array of garish rings."

"Manson will express his 'sincere' regret at the death of one of Scotland's finest academics and declare himself devastated that the police should think that he or any of his associates could have had anything to do with such an unspeakable crime! Besides, as the super must surely know, 'the Mansons have no business interests in Edinburgh', allegedly. And there, I fear, the interview and our investigation will probably end."

By the time John finished his story, both nurses were making increasingly agitated signs that the visit should be over, and he reluctantly left to re-join his wheelchair, promising to be back later.

The next few days passed in a haze for Anya. Her jaw and eye socket were healing well and the heavy bruising on her left side was slowly beginning to fade. The long knife wound on her leg was a different matter. It was infected and heavy doses of intravenous antibiotic coupled with intravenous morphine were doing little for her powers of concentration.

"Assassins really should have the decency to sterilise their knives before sticking them into people," she mused to the nurse who was painstakingly changing the dressing on her leg.

John spent a lot of time at her bedside, bringing her up to date with what was happening and arrangements for getting everyone home.

"The British Consul General called at the hospital yesterday but I told her you were not well enough for a visit yet, which was true. Also, I wasn't sure how you would feel about an encounter with a representative of your former employer. Anyway, she left her card and I said we would be in touch if we needed any assistance."

Anya smiled, then instantly regretted it as her jaw issued a silent, but severe reprimand.

"I will have to take Niall back to UK on Tuesday." Registering the bemused expression on Anya's face, John added, "That's in two days' time, this is Sunday."

"It's amazing how quickly you can lose track of time when you are drugged to the eyeballs. But how on earth will you manage to accompany Niall with one shoulder strapped to your chest. You can't help him into and out of his wheelchair or push it with just one arm!"

"Faisal will take us to the airport and, believe it or not, we both qualify for special assistance on this trip. Also, I need to get back to brief my super on the fine detail of all that has happened here. Attempting to type a report with my left hand has proved to be a major challenge."

"The good news is that Kadir has extracted some useful information from Hans Peter about his contact with the Manson brothers and this might just help us to nail them, or at least one of them, on a charge of conspiracy to murder Charles Gibson. It won't be easy, they will be lawyered up to the hilt and any of their associates who might be tempted to help the police with their enquiries will run the risk of meeting the same fate as Dr Gibson."

"Does that risk also apply to the investigating officer?" Anya asked in mounting alarm. "Surely that's a job for the Strathclyde police, not for you; you are supposed to retire in a month's time in any case."

"The Strathclyde police will certainly be very interested in the case, but the murder, unfortunately, took place in Edinburgh. I'll be back at the weekend to see how you are doing."

"You can't keep flying to and from Istanbul just because of me," Anya said, not meaning a word of it. The response was immensely reassuring.

"Try to stop me!"

Anya felt strangely bereft after John and Niall left her on the Monday afternoon. Niall looked frail but his indomitable sense of humour was as much in evidence as ever.

"Anya, this man doesn't even begin to know how to look after you. You must promise to come to Edinburgh as soon as they let you out of here so that I can take over and keep you safe."

Her next visitor took her completely by surprise. She was aware of a flurry of activity in the corridor outside her room just before the policeman on duty poked his head round the door to announce that the British Ambassador was outside. Would it be all right to let him in? Before she had a chance to reply, a large man bearing an enormous bunch of flowers appeared in the doorway.

He sported an unruly mop of sandy coloured hair turning white at the temples and, in contrast to traditional ambassadorial attire, an immaculate Harris Tweed jacket over a pair of stylish cords. Brilliant blue eyes and a disarming smile broke down the last of Anya's defences.

"Our Consul General was sent packing the other day by a very determined Scottish policeman. I thought it only fair that on our second attempt to visit you, I should present myself for rejection in her stead! I am Donald Mackie."

In spite of herself, Anya laughed.

"It certainly never occurred to me as I was being unceremoniously thrown out through a back door in King Charles Street two years ago, that my next encounter with the FCO would be an ambassador bearing flowers!"

"Aha! One should always be wary of ambassadors bearing gifts! To be serious for a moment, we are very proud of what you have done and I am pleased to see that you are on the mend and being well looked after."

He spoke in a lilting Scottish accent lightly modulated by Oxford or Cambridge and years spent in the service of Her Majesty overseas. Anya warmed to him.

The next twenty minutes flew by in animated conversation, at the conclusion of which Anya couldn't help asking, "Did my former ambassador's career ever recover?"

"Ah, Everett! He is retired now and I believe spends most of his time propping up the bar at The Athenaeum Club regaling the unwary with tales of how he had single-handedly unmasked a plot by an Iranian master spy to entrap a British diplomat. Apparently, the British public owes him a debt of gratitude for his brilliance in uncovering this threat to national security and enabling everyone to sleep soundly in bed at night."

"That's not quite how I remember it!"

"I have always believed there might be another version of events, as does virtually everyone else in the Service! Look, I can scarcely imagine how awful that experience must have been for you, and how difficult you must find dealing with former colleagues, but I hope you will accept my card with my personal contact numbers."

"I know you are being well looked after by John Arbuthnot, but please do not hesitate to call me if I can be of help. You are a brave woman, but even brave women need a helping hand sometimes!"

With that, he left.

Chapter 21
Six Days Later

Anya woke to the sound of a gentle knock on the bedroom door, announcing the arrival of Afnan, the Demercol's maid. A delicious aroma of coffee and hot Turkish flat bread accompanied Afnan into the room. "Bonjour, Madame. Ça va bien?" She asked in halting French—the only language they had in common—as she set out a breakfast of eggs, fruit, coffee and bread on a table by the window.

"Très bien, merci, Afnan," the traditional response being far from the truth on this final morning as a guest of the Demercol family. Ayşe Demercol had taken charge of Anya on her release from hospital four days earlier, and for four days she had been treated like royalty by the whole family. Today, she would have to leave this beautiful guest room with its large, comfortable bed, rich carpeting and elegant furnishings.

Over breakfast, she would watch for the last time as the gossamer mist over the Bosphorus melted away in the early morning sunshine. This morning, she would have to say 'goodbye' to the wonderful people who had looked after her so well following the attempt on her life. This evening, she would be back in a small, dark flat in Southend-on-Sea, alone.

She had reached the end of six tempestuous and at times terrifying weeks; an action-packed adventure in the company of people she had come to care for—come to love, she realised, in the case of John Arbuthnot. Unbidden tears welled at the thought she might never see John again. He had certainly been very protective of her ever since that first evening in Edinburgh, protective to the point of risking his life for her, but wasn't that what policemen did?

They put themselves on the line to protect members of the public, especially members of the public who were in possession of critical evidence in a multiple murder case, not to mention holding the key to recovering stolen works of art! She had been foolish to hope that he had being doing anything other than his job.

"There's something I need to discuss with you," John said as he helped her negotiate the angled, wooden staircase leading down to the living area of the villa, a major challenge to a novice on crutches.

"The UK Culture Minister has been in touch and she and the Minister of Defence would like to meet us to offer their congratulations on our role in putting Hans Peter von Seidel behind bars. They originally suggested a meeting later today but I said that was out of the question, you would be exhausted and sore after travelling."

"They have come back to me suggesting a meeting at noon tomorrow and have offered to book a hotel near Westminster for us. I asked if the press would be there, knowing the answer before I posed the question, and have been reassured that it would simply be a photo opportunity. I told them I would need to ask if you felt up to it and that if you said 'no' then that would be final."

Anya laughed. "How like politicians to want the photoshoot while the story is still front-page news. Well, OK then as long as they arrange a really good hotel and are prepared to wait till mid-day. It takes me a long time to get going in the mornings at the moment."

What she didn't say was that the idea of spending one more evening with John was worth the stress of facing the cameras while her face still showed the signs of Hans Peter's handiwork. It also postponed the moment when she would have to return to her drab little flat.

The scale of the photo opportunity took them both by surprise. It was held in the function room of the hotel in which they were staying. More than half the floor space was taken up by cameramen and journalists, none paying the least bit of attention to the efforts of a red-faced press officer tasked to keep them under control.

Cameras flashed as soon as Anya and John entered the room, much to Anya's annoyance. She had not yet fully mastered crutches and dreaded to think what her clumsy efforts would look like on screen. The two ministers who awaited them were not alone. The Head of the Armed Forces, the Chief Rabbi and the Director of the National Gallery were also in attendance.

The ministers' words of welcome and congratulation were all but drowned out by a barrage of questions from the press, until John reached for a microphone and, with a calm authority borne of long experience, brought the pack to order, recalling that, as seasoned pros, they must know that nothing could be said until the multiple charges against Hans Peter von Seidel had been properly investigated and brought before the relevant courts.

Coffee and soft drinks were brought in as soon as the press corps left—all, that is, apart from the Head of Broadcasting at the BBC. The BBC planned to produce a prime-time documentary as soon as legal restrictions were lifted, they would be in touch. The army planned to hold a ceremony at Le Paradis to commemorate the British prisoners of war who were gunned down there; they hoped Anya and John would attend.

The Art world, still reeling from the news of so many lost masterpieces re-emerging into the light of day, would honour the role played by Anya and John at a future date. When that date might be was anyone's guess as the task of authenticating each stolen item, checking its provenance and tracing owners and heirs would not be simple.

The Jewish Community planned to hold a major event to mark the capture of a man who had destroyed millions of Jewish lives in pursuit of a deranged ideology and unbridled greed.

Over a quiet lunch in a nearby Italian restaurant, Anya and John smiled at each other in bemused silence.

Chapter 22
International Airport, Doha

Amir Rashid looked despondently at the departure board indicating that his Iran Air flight back to Teheran was delayed by two hours. After much political and bureaucratic equivocation, he had finally been given permission to accept the invitation to speak at an international conference in Doha on the treatment of childhood cancers.

Confident that Dr Rashid was safely secured in the departure lounge, Amir's Iranian 'minder' had wandered off in search of some distraction to fill the time before their flight, and anything would be more entertaining than sitting beside his morose, silent charge for several hours. Alone for the first time that day, Amir settled down for the prolonged wait.

The imminent departure of a scheduled flight to Rome brought powerful memories rushing back—memories of Anya and of the hopes he once held for a future together; and evoking the thousand regrets which still inhabited his waking hours.

On the seat facing him, a young man in a crumpled business suit slept fitfully, a large carry-on bag at his feet tagged for Sydney. Lost in his thoughts, Amir had not been listening to the announcements until a final call in Arabic for the Sydney flight broke into his thoughts. He crossed over to the young man and gingerly tapped him on the shoulder.

"Excuse me, Sir, but I couldn't help noticing the Sydney tag on your bag and Qatar Airways has just announced the final call for your flight."

The young businessman woke with a start and, grabbing his bag, coat and laptop, thanked Amir profusely in polished, public school English as he set off at speed towards his departure gate, coat and laptop bag swaying wildly in his wake. Amir allowed himself a wry smile. All was not perfect in the West.

It would seem that the City of London was still flogging its young hopefuls to the point of utter exhaustion. It was only then that Amir noticed that the young man had dropped his half-read copy of *The Telegraph*. Convincing himself rather guiltily that an unfit fifty year old had no chance of catching up with the newspaper's fleet footed owner, Amir grasped the rare opportunity to get a western perspective on world affairs.

Checking that his 'minder' was nowhere in sight, Amir turned to the front page and let out an audible gasp as he stared at the main photograph in utter disbelief. It was Anya, surrounded by British Government ministers, police and other dignitaries. She looked pale and thin, with dark marks around one eye and a heavily bandaged leg just visible beneath the hem of loose, Turkish-style trousers.

Struggling to concentrate, he read the synopsis of an incredible story, his attention unerringly drawn to the tall man looking protectively down at Anya. In dismay, he recognised that the policeman's fond look conveyed far more than a professional concern for a key witness. Whether the affection was mutual he could not tell as Anya was looking straight ahead at the camera.

As he read the full three page spread given over to the story of a strange ring which had been the key to unravelling war crimes, murder and art theft on a truly monumental scale, disbelief gave way to alternating waves of despair and relief—despair that Anya was forever lost to him, and relief that she was safe.

A sudden idea briefly steadied his whirling mind. He could write to her now, care of *The Telegraph,* and ask the young barista in the café to post the letter from Doha for him. A Qatari postmark would not endanger her. The thought dissolved as quickly as it had appeared. What could he say?

That he loved her, had always loved her and was desperately sorry for what he had done to her? She would find that hard to believe. That he lived in the hope that one day relations between their two countries would improve to the extent that a former Iranian spy found guilty of entrapping a British diplomat would be granted a visa to join her anywhere in the western world? That was never going to happen.

A letter from him could only unsettle Anya, and if opened by others, could make her situation even worse. He had no idea how long he sat in helpless silence as unchecked tears rolled down his cheeks, drawing sympathetic or simply curious looks from fellow travellers.

When at last his flight was called, he rose slowly to his feet, stuffed the newspaper into a nearby bin and set off wearily in search of his 'minder' and the departure gate for Teheran. All the unrealistic hope that had sustained him since his abrupt departure from Rome had gone.

Chapter 23
Bearsden, Glasgow

Three and a half thousand miles away, a small group of men sat round a table reading the same, alarming story in *The Glasgow Herald.*

"I always knew that your heavy drinking and bloody stupidity would land us all in serious trouble one day," Rikki Manson growled at his youngest brother. "Whatever made you agree to a contract made in a whisky stupor in a bar in Tangier, for fuck's sake?"

"I don't remember you objecting at the time given how much money was involved," Ron Manson replied petulantly. "And how was I to know that a man calling himself Josef Schmidt was a wanted war criminal called von Seider?"

"Von Seidel! The man's name is von *Seidel!* The least you could do is get his name straight. And if I am right, two years on from your bungled attempt to extract information from Charles Gibson, the second and largest payment for our services has still not arrived in our off-shore account."

"Stop it both of you!" Reg Manson cut into the heated exchange. "There is no point in fighting over past history. We need to focus on how we ensure that no trace of evidence can lead the police back to us."

"Why would anyone suspect we had anything to do with Gibson's death anyway?" Ron asked, naively.

"Have you forgotten already? I was interviewed by Lothian and Borders Police two weeks ago and, I don't mind telling you, that upset me. They suspect our involvement, or at least Arbuthnot does."

"But you said the police were just on a fishing expedition, they had no evidence linking us to the death. And what's Arbuthnot got to do with it anyway, it was his super who called?"

"Because Arbuthnot is behind all this and he has always suspected we had a hand in Gibson's murder. What have you not understood in all you have just read about his part in the hunt for von Seidel? He has always made it plain that he will not rest until he has solved Gibson's murder, and while we sit here arguing, von Seidel is probably singing like a canary in a Turkish jail."

"I expect a call from Arbuthnot at any moment now that he is back in UK. We need to think carefully and fast."

"Ron, are you absolutely certain that von Seidel never knew your real name or anything about our family business?" Rikki asked.

"No, I gave him a false name. The payment to seal the contract was made in cash as you know, and the second one was to be to our numbered account overseas. The contact number he had for me was for a pay-as-you-go phone registered in my false name."

"Where is that phone now?"

"I got rid of it six months ago when I realised Schmidt's—von Seider's—phone was no longer active. The phone I used is somewhere in the River Clyde, and the sim card was incinerated along with our late uncle Mack at Maryhill Crematorium in August!"

"Did von *Seidel* know you were from Glasgow?" Reg asked, disregarding the rather gruesome account of the destruction of the sim card.

"No, I told him I was from Edinburgh, that's why he gave us the contract."

Four days later, Strathclyde police responded to a report of a car partially submerged in deep water at one of the lonelier stretches around Loch Lomond. The bodies of two men had been recovered from the vehicle which had been stolen from a car park in Kirkintilloch earlier that day.

The police spokesman said that a thorough investigation of the road and the banks of the loch had been carried out, but it was too early to say what had caused the car to leave the road and plunge into the loch. In response to a journalist's question, he confirmed that the car's occupants were known to the police but that he could not comment further while the investigation was ongoing.

What neither the police nor the journalists could know was that key evidence linking the Manson brothers to the murder of Charles Gibson had also drowned in the loch that day.

Chapter 24
Southend-on-Sea

It was late afternoon, and already getting dark as John and Anya's taxi drew up outside the block of flats where Anya lived. As he helped her out of the taxi, John scanned the surrounding area with a professional eye, taking in the narrow, poorly lit streets and the unkempt high-rise buildings, the scuffed paintwork on the main entrance to Anya's block and the rattling lift with its lingering odour of stale sweat and cigarettes.

He didn't like what he saw. Years of experience of life in the run down back streets of cities told him that this was not a safe place for Anya. In truth, this assessment sat rather well with thoughts he had been harbouring for some time about where Anya might live in the future. It would strengthen his case when he found the right moment to propose a move to Edinburgh.

He was sensitive enough to know that Anya was not ready to contemplate a permanent relationship yet, and he knew that they both needed time to get to know each other in more normal circumstances, thus he could have jumped for joy when Niall Chambers made a suggestion which might, just might, provide a solution.

Entering Anya's flat was like entering a different world. Soft lighting spread a welcoming glow around the living area. The room was attractively furnished in an Italianate style with a compact kitchen and dining area at the far end.

John carried Anya's suitcase along the narrow hallway leading to her bedroom and left it as requested at the foot of the double bed, admiring the rich Italian brocade of the bed cover and curtains, and the intricately carved mahogany dresser and bedside tables which completed the furnishing in the room.

The walls were adorned with fine prints of Rome and photographs of friends and family were displayed on all available surfaces. He moved over to the window to close the curtains and looked out onto a very different scene. Down below, a litter-strewn courtyard adjoined two blocks of flats.

Weeds grew up through discoloured concrete flags and, amongst the accumulated junk, a rusting washing machine vied for space with a discarded bedstead. This was no place for Anya and he hoped that other tenants were unaware of the relative luxury of her home.

John found Anya staring out of the kitchen window as the last glimmer of light left the winter sky. Tears filled her eyes as she faced the reality of returning to a life constrained by futile visits to the Job Centre and constant worry about money—a life without John and the friends she had made through him; a life seemingly without purpose.

She was barely aware of John coming towards her and gently pulling her into his arms. To her embarrassment, she started crying, her head buried against his chest. Stroking her hair, he gently moved her head to the other side of his chest making her tears turn to apologetic laughter as she realised she had been nuzzling into his bullet wound.

"Is there a branch of Marks and Spencer near here? While you sort things out, I could go and get a bottle of wine and something nice for us to eat."

"I thought you were going back to Edinburgh tonight," Anya said, barely daring to hope that she had heard correctly.

"I've changed my mind. If I catch an early train from Southend Victoria in the morning, I can be in Edinburgh by mid-afternoon. My super is unlikely to fire me three weeks before I retire and after all we have been through! I'll sleep on the sofa if you will allow that."

Over a relaxed dinner, John told Anya about Niall's request.

"Niall has been in hospital since he returned from Istanbul and doctors have said he is no longer fit to live on his own. They have asked Social Work to find a suitable Nursing Home for him. You can imagine how Niall feels about that! The only other possibility is that he finds someone to live with him."

"Care assistants could come to the house to wash and dress him and attend to his physical needs, but he would need someone to cook, check that he takes his medication, shop for him and be there to summon help if needed. He asked me to ask you if you would be prepared to be that person."

"He says it would not be for long—he has been given three to six months to live, and that he would leave a glowing reference for you with his lawyer so that you never need to use the Foreign Office reference ever again."

"You don't need to answer straight away. I am hoping you will let me come back at the weekend to take you to

Edinburgh for as long as you like, and you can visit Niall and discuss it with him."

"I have made up my mind, and the answer is yes. You can let Niall know immediately as the prospect of a Nursing Home must be terrifying him. I would love to come to Edinburgh at the weekend, but I am sure I will be able to travel on my own by then. It would be madness for you to come all the way down here, just to turn round and go back."

"Madness it may be, but that is just what is going to happen. You get yourself into too much trouble if you are left on your own and you will have heavy luggage. My car is an automatic, so there is no problem about driving and we could break the journey back at Durham or York if you would like that."

Next morning, John tiptoed into Anya's room and kissed her lightly on the forehead.

"I am going now. I'll call you tonight and I'll be back on Friday afternoon. Please take care while I am away."

As the door closed behind him, Anya remembered the last time a man she loved left promising to return. This time would be different, she tried to reassure herself.

Chapter 25
Bearsden, Glasgow

Arbuthnot braked abruptly outside the pillared entrance to the Manson villa, sending flurries of displaced gravel in all directions. He got out of the car smiling quietly at the careless angle at which he had parked, flagrantly disregarding the neat rows of box interspersed with expensive ornamental stone delineating the parking spaces in which callers were meant to position their vehicles.

He took the broad, stone steps two at a time, striding past the henchman at the front door with barely a nod.

"Reg in his usual lair?" He asked the flustered henchman chasing after him.

"Mr Manson is waiting for you in the library, Sir."

Reg and Ronnie Manson were sitting in strained silence as Arbuthnot entered the large room, its garish pretentions to grandeur at odds with the unusually dishevelled looks of its occupants. Ronnie's face had the unhealthy yellowish tinge of the habitual drinker; Reg's was suffused with the bluish red blotches of cardiac disease compounded by barely suppressed anger.

"And to what do we owe the pleasure of the second visit in two weeks from Lothian and Borders Police?" Reg asked, the forced smile at odds with his wary, calculating eyes.

"I thought I might bring you up to date with our investigation into the death of Charles Gibson. Much has happened since my superintendent called on you, and it seemed only right to let you know," Arbuthnot replied with the ghost of a smile.

"As I told your superintendent in no uncertain terms, I have no idea why you people think we had anything to do with that unpleasant business. We had nothing to do with the death of Charles Gibson, so this is a wasted journey, Arbuthnot. In any case, I hear you are about to retire."

"Quite so, but the investigation goes on you'll be pleased to hear. You will be aware that the Turkish police have arrested a friend of yours, Ronnie, Hans Peter von Seidel. Of course, I forgot—you know him better as Josef Schmidt, Joe Smith. Not a very original pseudonym, Ronnie. That should have told you to be more cautious."

"What the fuck are you on about, Arbuthnot? How on earth would Ronnie know a Nazi?" Reg shouted, the unhealthy-looking red blotches intensifying on his neck and face.

"Ah, it all goes back to a whisky drinking session in a bar in Tangier, isn't that right, Ronnie? An evening when you agreed to arrange a little roughing up and robbery at the home of Charles Gibson; not to mention the onward transmission of an item your buddy, Josef Schmidt, was anxious to lay his hands on. Twenty grand was the deal, wasn't it?"

"Five grand paid up front in cash and the rest to a numbered off-shore account on successful completion. Of course, the task wasn't completed successfully, was it, Ronnie? Charles Gibson ended up dead and your boys didn't find the all-important item. No wonder the balance remains outstanding."

"Enough of this crap!" Reg spluttered in rage. "Ronnie was never in a bar in Tangier; anyway Tangier's in a Muslim country? There are no bars in Muslim countries."

"Ah, there I regret to disabuse you, Reg. You should travel more. There are always bars if you know where to look, with the possible exception of Saudi Arabia perhaps. And we all know that if there's a bar to be found, we can always count on Ronnie to find it. Unfortunately, Ronnie, von Seidel remembers the evening rather well."

"Of course, he wasn't drinking as heavily as you and later in the evening after the contract was agreed, he was most entertained by your tales of the family's business activities. I don't suppose he ever showed you the nice photograph he took of you drinking at the bar, a pity—it's always good to have mementos of foreign travels, don't you think? I have brought a copy just to remind you."

Arbuthnot slid the photograph across the coffee table. "Von Seidel is a careful man and he wanted to be sure he had evidence against you, should anything go wrong with your little arrangement."

"All that proves is that I was in the bar, not that I was with this Nazi character you appear to be obsessed with," Ron said, a desperate edge to his thin voice.

"One of the wonders of digital photography is that a date appears on the lower edge of a photograph. Now the date on this photo coincides with dates when my good friends at The Home Office confirm that your passport was used to travel to

Morocco—a few days of fun with Moroccan boys, was it, Ron? They tell me that bar is famous for it."

"The date also coincides with a brief visit to Morocco by von Seidel who is not known for an interest in boys. Women are more to his liking, second only to his passion for violence, art theft and murder on an industrial scale, of course."

Reg looked as if he was on the verge of having a seizure. "What are you insinuating, Arbuthnot?" He shouted, banging his fist on the desk. "First you accuse Ron of being involved in a murder plot with a Nazi war criminal, and now that he is a fucking fairy!"

"Oh, I'm sure Ron will be able to explain everything to you once I have gone," Arbuthnot replied airily. "Now, if you don't mind, I'll have that photo back, please."

"Photos can be doctored!" Reg said icily. "I'm calling my lawyer right now."

"No need for that, Reg. As I said, this is simply a courtesy call, and I wouldn't want to drag Giulio Cacciari away from his tireless efforts to defend the indefensible in Glasgow's law courts. I can almost hear his outraged tones if we went to court with what we have at the moment.

Surely, Your Honour, we cannot ask the court to accept as evidence a statement taken from a man under interrogation in a Turkish prison—a man who would surely say anything that might mitigate his desperate situation…

We should also be aware that the Turkish police may feel they owe a debt to Lothian and Borders Police because of the assistance provided by Chief Inspector Arbuthnot in the capture of a man wanted for at least three murders, and in the recovery of a vast horde of stolen art, all on Turkish soil. We cannot, therefore, dismiss the possibility that Turkish interrogators might extort confessions to fit Arbuthnot's purposes.

"I just want you both to know, that we are still collecting evidence...something for you to think about on sleepless nights. No doubt my colleagues will be in touch sooner or later."

With that, Arbuthnot rose to leave.

"Oh, I almost forgot, my condolences on the untimely death of your two associates at Loch Lomond the other day. A treacherous stretch of road, that."

"Go to hell, Arbuthnot!"

"See you there," Arbuthnot replied with a grin as he left the room. Half way along the corridor, he stopped and turned to the henchman escorting him from the premises.

"Sorry. Just realised I left my pen on the coffee table."

As he approached the library door, he heard Reg yelling, "Get out of my sight, Ronnie, and don't leave this house until I decide what to do about you!" A terrified Ronnie ran from the room just as Arbuthnot entered to retrieve his pen. Reg rewarded Arbuthnot's apology with a furious glare.

Arbuthnot smiled as he climbed back into his car and drove away, the clang of security gates closing ringing in his ears as he exited the Manson's property. An unmarked van parked on the opposite side of the road moved off following Arbuthnot's car for several miles before pulling into a supermarket car park behind him.

Arbuthnot got out of his car and climbed into the van to be greeted by two detectives from Strathclyde police.

"Did you get all that?" Arbuthnot asked, wincing as he pulled the wire off his bare chest.

"Every last, sweet word," said Detective Sergeant David Wylie. "Inadmissible in court, of course as it wasn't recorded under caution, but very useful in helping us to link the Loch Lomond case to the Mansons. I visited the partner of one of the deceased yesterday."

"Three kids and another on the way, so not a happy lady. Said her man used to do jobs for Ronnie Manson from time to time, but not since Ronnie refused to pay out over a bungled job in Edinburgh two years ago. I thought that might interest you!"

Epilogue

Niall died at the end of May, five months after Anya had taken over as his personal assistant and primary carer. A warm summer sun bathed the well-tended gardens at Mortonhall Crematorium where friends and associates had gathered to say farewell to a popular and highly respected man.

As tributes flowed to the loveable, delightfully eccentric friend and gifted goldsmith, Anya tussled with a whirlwind of conflicting emotions—sadness at the loss of a person she had come to care for very deeply and relief that his suffering was over. As the last of the mourners headed off to enjoy a traditional Scottish wake, Niall's lawyer approached her.

"Could you call at my office some time tomorrow?" He asked with a hint of a smile. "Niall has left me with some very specific instructions with regard to you."

True to his word, Niall had left a reference for Anya which, as John later remarked, would have qualified her for a job as PA to the Queen. But that wasn't all. The lawyer passed over a hand-written instruction from Niall to transfer a sum of money immediately to Anya 'so that she can find a proper place to live'.

"Why on earth has he left fifty thousand pounds to me?" Anya stammered in an utter confusion of surprise and disbelief. "That's an absolute fortune, surely there must be some mistake!"

"Indeed, there is a mistake," the lawyer replied, laughing gently. "I think you'll find you have overlooked a zero. The sum is five hundred thousand."

Anya just stared at the lawyer in wordless amazement.

"Although, he lived relatively modestly, Niall was a very wealthy man. Most of his estate will go to various charities, but this is left to you, and I quote, 'to thank you for saving him from a nursing home, for your friendship, your care and the intellectual stimulus you brought to his final months'. He would not have missed the Istanbul adventure for worlds."

In late summer, Anya closed the door of her flat in Southend-on-Sea for the last time. She and John would continue to live in Edinburgh until they found somewhere nearer to friends and to John's daughter and grandchildren in London. Their initial forays into the property market in and around London had been depressing.

Most of the places they had looked at had been in cramped, commuter developments with little or no garden, no community hub or parkland nearby. The places they did like were either beyond their combined budget, or so far from London they would be as well staying in Edinburgh. As Anya handed over the keys of the Southend flat at the estate agency in the High Street, she noticed a large display of properties for sale.

One of them immediately caught her eye. It was a five roomed Victorian cottage with a large garden, situated at the end of a cul-de-sac in Leigh-on-Sea. In one photograph, she could see woodland beyond the back garden and, from another angle, the bell tower of an ancient church. The house was described as 'located in an idyllic setting, structurally sound, but in need of some modernisation'.

The price was well within their budget though doubtless the 'modernisation' would involve a further substantial outlay.

Anya fell in love with the cottage at first glance. A lone, pink hollyhock stood sentinel over its fallen comrades below a large bay window, and a riotous red ornamental poppy sprawled carelessly over the path to the front door. Anya barely listened to the estate agent's well-rehearsed sales pitch as she wandered around the cottage.

Elegant fireplaces in the two front rooms retained their original Victorian tiling, and fine cornices surrounded the walls and ceilings. She was vaguely aware of the estate agent extolling the 'many fine period features' as she contemplated the rooms. An old fashioned Aga and a large deal table held pride of place in the kitchen.

For a brief moment, Anya imagined she saw a young girl with long brown hair hunched over her homework at the table, while a slim, grey haired woman prepared food beside the Aga. A vivid memory of Amir's boyish laughter caught her by surprise. He had teased her about her ability to conjure up images of people from the past in historic settings.

She pulled herself back to the present in mild irritation. Why did memories of Amir still intrude? Why were they always of good times they had shared? Why, if she had to remember him at all, was it not about his devastating betrayal of her? Today she was viewing a house that she might one day share with a much finer man. Focus on that!

She followed the estate agent out through French windows onto a patio overlooking the rear garden. At the far end, a gate in the old stone wall opened out onto a path to the woodland beyond. Anya walked down the short flight of steps leading from the small patio onto a large expanse of uncut grass on which an old-fashioned swing swayed in the breeze.

Anya imagined she saw the girl again, her long brown hair blowing across her face, laughing as the swing rose higher and higher. The estate agent broke into her reverie, suggesting that she might want to see the rest of the house. Together they climbed the curved staircase to the first floor. From the master bedroom window, she could see the ancient church tower soaring above the roof tops.

In one of the smaller bedrooms, she opened a wall cupboard and found a neatly tied bundle of school reports for a girl called Catherine Mitchell. She had been told that the previous owner of the house was a Miss Agnes Mitchell. Was Catherine a sister? No, the dates were a generation out, yet it would have been unusual in Miss Mitchell's day for a single woman to bring up a child on her own.

She replaced the school reports and closed the cupboard door, suddenly aware that the estate agent was hovering nearby looking anxiously at his watch. He apologised, but would need to leave soon for another appointment. Thanking him at the front gate, Anya said she would make her own way back.

An elderly woman was tending roses in the garden next door, and on impulse, Anya called out to her. Did she know how to contact the Catherine Mitchell whose school reports she had found in the cottage.

"Oh yes, she lives in Edinburgh now. She was brought up by her aunt Agnes from the age of eight, after her mother died. No one knew who her father was. I miss Agnes. She was a fine woman and a good friend to me for over fifty years. Catherine didn't want to sell the house after Agnes died, but her husband had other ideas, preferred the idea of a holiday house in France apparently!"

"Are you thinking of buying the house? It would be so nice to have people living in it again. I was just going to make some tea, would you like some?"

"That would be lovely, thank you. I am Anya Wilson, by the way."

"Edith Masterton; pleased to meet you."

While tea was being made, Anya phoned John. "How quickly can you get here? I think I might have found our house."

Printed in Great Britain
by Amazon